MW00533063

NIGHT OFFICE

ASSET RESOURCE MANAGEMENT

NIGHT OFFICE

BEYOND THE WALLS OF SANITY

COMPILED BY **MARK TEPPO**

ASSET RESOURCE MANAGEMENT	
APS−481/q	FOR INTERNAL USE ONLY

51325 Books

Produced in association with **51325 Books** and Firebird Creative, LLC (Clackamas, OR).

Sometimes the voices in your head are right . . .

A Night Office publication
ARM – APS – 481/q
rev. 12/ ed. 03.2021

http://nightoffice.org

ASSET RESOURCE MANAGEMENT

BEYOND THE WALLS OF SANITY

APS−481/q

SCOPE: This Advanced Psychological Strategies assessment measures the Mental Acuity & Psychological Stability of a field operative, and should be administered following the completion of a Night Office-sanctioned field operation. It encapsulates the creation of, management of, and dismissal of self-actuated therapeutic personalities, thereby allowing the Office of Psychological Investment Notarization & Emotional Analysis Legation to quantify a field operative's mental stability. All field operatives must be cleared by PINEAL before being allowed back into field operation rotation.

This assessment tests the integrity of various nth-dimensional sub-structures of the psychological matrices, as well as the field operative's neural flexibility and capacity for mental peregrinations without suffering psychotic degradation. Results from this exercise will be tabulated into a Mental Acuity and Psychological Stability score, which will be recorded in the field operative's Life Integrity Existential Schematic.

Commentary in regards to the relative success or failure of any given end point within this assessment is provided to downplay any lasting mental, emotional, physical, or psychological scarring that may result as having undergone this post-field operation assessment.

Night Office Asset Resource Management makes every effort to present these assessments in accordance with the most current policies, procedures, and practical applications of relevant esoteric knowledge, but Night Office Asset Resource Management offers no assurances that these materials are truly up-to-date.

Please ensure that your Willing & Ready Invocation (Form PALM-ISA-84/b) is up to date prior to undergoing this Advanced Psychological Strategies assessment.

DISCLAIMER: This Advanced Psychological Strategies assessment is intended to assess, judge, and quantify the mental stability of Asset Resource Management field operatives, and as such, will expose them to self-directed therapeutic personalities, as well as potentially hazardous secondary effects of exploring these self-awareness actuations, including but not limited to the creation of unexpected mental health stressors, the eructation of previously sublimated personality disorders, the resurgence of uncategorized phobias, irrational fears, and neurological tremors, tics, and fidgets. While Night Office Asset Resource Management has attempted to thoroughly address all possible scenarios and outcomes of these assessments, it is entirely likely that new stressors, hazards, neurological maladies, and other causes for psychotic breaks may present themselves as a result of, or during the process of, or in the aftermath of completing this assessment.

To the extend that local, state, and federal guidelines, mandates, and statutes regarding extra-terrestrial entities, cosmic fungi, and other non-Euclidean monstrosities even exist, Night Office Asset Resource Management makes no guarantee that procedures, policies, and practices as suggested in this assessment make any effort whatsoever to follow these existing guidelines, mandates, and statutes. Nor does Night Office Asset Resource Management assume any responsibility—implied, implicit, or suggested to the contrary—for psychological, physical, and/or mental damage, grief, or distress a field operative may incur as a result of, or during the process of, or in the aftermath of completing this assessment.

INSTRUCTIONS: This Night Office Asset Resource Management Advanced Psychological Strategies assessment is a series of interwoven narrative choices that are intended to chart the mental stability of an Asset Resource Management field operative. At the end of each passage within this assessment, you will be provided with a variety of narrative options. It is up to you to decide which path is the correct path. You should continue to explore the narrative branches until you reach an end point, whereupon you will be provided with a summary statement in regards to the assessment, as well as a Mental Acuity and Psychological Stability score.

Please refer to the Appendix upon completion of this assessment for further details about your MAPS score.

SHORT FORM ACKNOWLEDGMENT: The act of turning this page is a tacit acknowledgment on the part of the field operative that they are engaging in this assessment, and that they do so of their own volition, as per PALM-DLT-23/d.

Read & Understood: _____
[initials]

SECTION A

INTROSPECTION

A-1

This assessment is intended to quantify the current level of mental stability and holistic integrity of an Asset Resource Management field operative. It contains a variety of self-directed encounters with therapeutic personalities. It is an advanced visualization technique requiring exceptional intellectual rigor and a flexible acceptance of subjective reality. It is helpful if you had an imaginary friend as a child.

If you had an imaginary friend, **go to A-3**.

If you were not allowed imaginary friends, **go to A-2**.

A-2

A lack of imaginary friends suggests a lack of imagination across the board. When you're deep in the embrace of a Burbarken Warp Fold, fending off tentacled space cats from Xyullo, being able to think outside the box—rather than the persistent irreality you are currently encased in—is pretty darn useful.

This detail should have been noted in your Life Integrity Experience Schematic. Someone in Personal Acquisition & Liability Management didn't complete a Inclusive Risk Evaluation form (PALM—IRE—52/a) correctly. The Human Asset Naturalization Department will audit your Life Integrity Experience Schematic to discover who fucked that up, because, frankly, we probably shouldn't have let you out into the field in the first place.

Well, no matter about that now. You've seen things no one should have to see, especially someone with a rigid understanding of how the Universe operates. We'll just have to press on with this exercise and hope for the best, right?

Well, there was that one time when you did imaginative play about that person you were attracted to in college. Does that count?

Go to A-4.

Yeah, there's no way around it. You had a dull childhood, a mediocre adolescence, and a monochrome existence as an adult. Which is why you joined the Night Office, of course. You wanted something better, something stranger. We're sorry that we—ahem—went overboard on the strange shit index.

Would you believe us if we said that we can fix this?

Go to A-5.

A-3

Oh, excellent. The ability to fabricate and interact with imaginary friends is very helpful in this assessment. In fact, we're going to help you make a new imaginary friend. This one is a therapist. They're going to talk with you about your feelings in an effort to check on your mental state. You should treat them like all of your other imaginary friends.

The ones you used to douse with kerosene and set on fire? Those imaginary friends?
Go to A-8.

Well, this should be interesting because your imaginary friends typically spanked you when you had been naughty, and you were very, very naughty in that last field operation, weren't you?
Go to A-9.

Your last imaginary friend was a talking squirrel.
Go to A-10.

A-4

Self-directed sexytime dreams about someone else? Well, it's not what we meant when we asked if you had imaginary friends, but—in a pinch—it'll do.

And no, we don't need to know any more about those sorts of things. Keep them to yourself. Don't be weird.

Anyway, take a moment and remember how that felt. No, not that part. The other part—the part where you allowed yourself to imagine a conversation between you and someone else. It wasn't real, of course, but it could have been. This other person could have been making eye contract. They could have been listening intently to the words coming out of your mouth. They wouldn't have been judging your slipshod sentence structure or your lackluster metaphorical dowhatsits. They'd have been looking into your eyes—a little bit dreamily, perhaps. They were engaged, and you felt like you mattered for a few minutes.

Yes, that's what we're talking about. Feeling like you matter. It's an important element in grounding yourself. If you are seen, then you exist, and if you are a verifiable point of light on the grand map of the cosmos, well, then you can counter the forces of darkness and malign corruption.

This assessment is intended to check whether or not you can still be seen when it counts. Okay?

This makes sense. You think you are ready to begin the hard part now.
Go to A-22.

Wait. This wasn't the hard part?
Go to A-7.

A-5

How are we going to fix your current inability to create imaginary characters? Well, we'll roll through several roleplaying scenarios to help activate and jumpstart those sections of your brain. If you complete these scenarios readily and feel that you have been properly motivated and actualized to create therapeutic personalities, we shall continue with this assessment. If you feel these roleplaying scenarios have not provided you with the appropriate level of confidence in regards to making shit up with your brain, you may terminate this assessment immediately. Please report to LIMB where mental conditioning and memory blockers will be installed so as to wipe your history with the Night Office.

Trust us. It is better this way.

Are you ready for some roleplaying?

Yes.
Go to B-1.

Actually, you remember an imaginary friend you once had. His name was Turk McDurk. He was a turtle. He liked rhubarb and barbed wire fences. You used to sing duets together.
Go to A-16.

A-6

Oh, so you played with dolls. Did you invite them to tea? Did you dress them in gender appropriate clothing? Did you assign them various roles, like "Lookout," or "Interrogator," or "Bait"? Did you cry when one or more of them were taken from you? Do you think more fondly about them than you do the real people who you work with?

You know, the dolls talk about you when you're not around. They do.

No, sorry. We're kidding. We didn't mean that last bit. You don't need to discipline them.

Anyway, we've gotten off track here. We've established that you are capable of having imaginary friends. That's all we wanted to accomplish here. We didn't want to distress any portion of your psyche—well, no more than it is already stressed.

It's okay. Breathe deep. Calm down. Let's think about this assessment. It's going to be a simple conversation with your therapist. That's right. Dr. Nebuchenezzar. You can call him "Dr. Nebs." He won't mind. Go ahead and prepare yourself now. We're going to visit him in just a moment . . .

Go to Section C. When prompted, please select C-1.

A-7

No, no, this is the preamble. The "get to know you" part before we peel back the top of your skull and go routing around with a dull knife and a spoon. Are you nervous already? Oops. That'll make things more difficult.

Try to relax. There really isn't a wrong answer in this assessment, except those narrative paths which lead you to your doom. There are many of them, because this is a Night Office assessment. We like to be thorough in our examinations of our field operatives.

Are you concerned about what we might find when we do this psychological profile?

Yes.
Go to A-11.

Not at all.
Go to A-13.

A-8

We'd like to remind you that lighting people on fire—even imaginary, phantasmagoric, and oneiric individuals—demonstrates a lack of empathy that violates the Morality Clause of your employment contract with the Night Office. As per Subsection 18a of your Personal Invocation & Promissory Exhortation form (PALM—PIPE—87/es), use of naked aggression and physical violence is specifically reserved for non-human and extra-terrestrial predators, mindless chattel, slaved sycophants, and other aberrant intelligences.

Perhaps we misunderstood what you meant by what you said. How about we try that again?

Imaginary friends. Yes or no?

Yes.
Go to A-22.

No.
Go to A-28.

A-9

Oh, we're very good at reading between the lines, and there was a lot you left out in your report about what happened at the Zel——— house. No, don't be upset. If there was something amiss in your report, the Human Asset Naturalization Department would have already reached out and asked you to fill out a Operational Causation & Assessment report (HAND—OCA—33/q).

Your HAND—OCA—33/q was fine, by the way. Exemplary, in fact. Field operatives have license to self-censor their reports so as to keep the focus on the actual task at hand. The particulars are rarely important. We generally assume that if your team doesn't come back, it is because they fucked up and were devoured or mind flayed or taken over by space jellies. We don't need to know the particulars and we tend to believe field operatives on their reports.

It may not be the best policy, but it is the most honest policy. Some of what you do in order to save the world need not ever be written down.

A large portion of this assessment, in fact, is meant to ascertain your mental state in the wake of the field operation. How do you feel about what you had to do? How does it affect your ability to function well? Are you going to have trouble sleeping at night?

Speaking of which, we should get started on that assessment.

Go to Section C. You may choose any option.

A-10

Oh, you had a talking squirrel as an imaginary friend? What was the squirrel's name? Nutso? That's a fine name.

No, no. We're not judging you. A talking squirrel is very imaginative. It demonstrates a childlike innocence. This sort of resilience against peer pressure and societal insistence on conformity is a source of strength for you. We can see that. Very good.

Are you still talking with Nutso?

What? No.
Go to A-12.

Maybe. Does it matter?
Go to A-14.

A-11

Oh, you do have some concerns about what this psychological assessment might uncover? Is there something you neglected to tell us in your Introspective Summary & Isolated Schematization report (PALM—ISS—33/r)? Or is there something you left off your last Operation Assessment & Review (LIMB—OAR—12/r)?

There might be something you forgot to mention on your Introspective Summary & Isolated Schematization report (PALM—ISS—33/r).
Go to A-41.

Oh, the LIMB—OAR—12/r? You may have forgotten to turn that in. Whoops.
Go to A-40.

A-12

You're no longer in contact with your imaginary squirrel friend from childhood. What happened? Did you abandon this friend, or did you grow out of requiring this sort of companion?

No, this isn't a trap. We're genuinely curious. What happened to the talking squirrel?

Nothing happened. You just drifted apart.
Go to A-33.

You'd rather not talk about it.
Go to A-35.

A-13

You're not concerned? Very good. Then you won't mind if we get right to it then.

Let's do this.
Go to Section C.

No, wait. There is something you want to confess before we start.
Go to A-11.

A-14

No, no. It doesn't matter if your imaginary squirrel friend is still around. It's a coping mechanism, after all, and the Night Office does not judge in this regard. Whatever gets you through the day is valid. Working for the Night Office is stressful in a way that no one understands, right?

In fact, can we let you in on a little secret? Everyone has an imaginary friend. That's right. There isn't a single person working for the Night Office who doesn't have someone special they can talk to when they are all alone. It's okay. Feeling a little less alone makes the Universe less frightening, doesn't it?

Yeah, this helps.
Go to A-17.

You suspect this is a trap.
Go to A-27.

A-15

You do know why space jelly goo is sticky, don't you? Because it is an invasive parasite that wants to invade your brain and rewire your intelligence so that you worship one of the Great Old Ones. If you get it on your skin, it will try to enter your body through an available orifice. If you leave it on your skin long enough, it will permeate your dermis and get into your bloodstream. Once it is there, you are doomed.

Don't you remember this part of Orientation & Inoculation? No?

That's probably because the space jelly goo that is in your brain right now has already wiped that from your memory. What else have you forgotten?

Well, it doesn't matter. It's not like you're going to get that memory back.

NICE TRY, SPACE JELLY, BUT WE'RE SMARTER THAN THAT. PREPARE TO BE ERADICATED.

MAPS SCORE: 2

A-16

We don't believe this story about a turtle. You should try again. We feel like you are making this up. Are you? Why don't you try again. Tell us a better story about this fellow.

Turk McDurk used to live over in the culvert that ran under the dirt road that led to the highway. You played with him often. You made mud castles and chased dragonflies. He held you when your father killed that little lamb on your thirteen birthday. He stroked your hair. You liked the way he stroked your hair.

Well . . . we're not entirely convinced.
Go to A-18.

All right, then. Turk McDurk it is. Excellent. Let's press on.
Go to A-20.

A-17

Oh, good. We're glad to provide some assistance. Yes, we're all a bat-shit crazy. We'd have to be, wouldn't we? Seeing the things we see. Doing the things we do. All that blood.

So much blood, right? It's hard to get out of clothing. And the ichor. That's the worst.

No, wait. Space jelly goo. That's the worst to get out, isn't it?

It is! So sticky.
Go to A-15.

This feels like another trap.
Go to A-42.

A-18

It would be helpful if there was some sort of record—some manner of external data—that could help us verify the existence of . . . It doesn't matter, really. In fact, if you are lying to us about this, all the better. That demonstrates an active imagination. That's all we were really looking for here, anyway.

Let's get to the assessment, shall we? Your therapist is named Dr. Nebuchenezzar. "Dr. Nebs," for short. He's waiting for you in his office. Can you see it in your head? That's right. Visualize it.

Okay, are you ready?

Go to Section C. When prompted, please select C-3.

A-19

Now why would you think this is a trap? We're merely trying to judge your state of mind before the full assessment starts. We asked a simple question: do you have imaginary friends? Either you do, or you don't. Getting defensive suggests you are hiding something from us.

You're not hiding anything.
Go to A-21.

Fuck off. You're done talking about Nutso.
Go to A-23.

A-20

We're not fooled, by the way. "Turk McDurk"? You should work on your made-up names. They're not very clever. Not a day goes by when we don't interact with someone who is lying to us. We're very good at spotting those who are hiding something.

Anyway, let's not get caught up in that right now. We have an important assessment to complete. Come along. Your therapist, Dr. Nebuchenezzar, is waiting for you. Dr. Nebs is swell. You'll like him. Probably as much as you like this Turk McDurk fellow.

Go to Section C.

A-21

Well, we think you're hiding something.

Go to Section C. When prompted, please select C-2.

A-22

Excellent. Imaginary friends are lovely. The next portion of this assessment is going to be like those times you spent with your imaginary friends. Relax and let your mind go blank. We're going to shift you over to the therapy session that will make up the bulk of this assessment.

Your therapist is named Dr. Nebuchenezzar, though many folks call him "Dr. Nebs." He's a gentle soul. Not like the Old Man. Dr. Nebs is very competent, so don't mistake his complacency and geniality as signs of weakness. This man will stab you if he thinks it is vital for your therapy.

(Where is the knife?)

Not literally. Metaphorically. Or, perhaps, spiritually. But not physically. The Night Office doesn't engage in such techniques anymore.

Anyway, Dr. Nebs is waiting for you in his office. That's right. His door is right over there. You can walk right through it. Don't mind the brief moment of dizziness and disorientation. That is normal.

Everything is normal, in fact. It's a perfectly lovely day. If there was more time, we'd recommend a walk in the park before you visit your therapist. A little fresh air does wonders for the brain.

Anyway, off you go. Good luck.

Go to Section C.

A-23

Oh, did we hit a nerve? Is Nutso chattering at you right now? Are you feeling agitated? Do you want to check the doors and windows? Go ahead. This assessment can wait. We want you to be calm and centered before you go any farther.

Doors locked? Windows secure? Good. Good. How is Nutso doing? Is he still chattering away? Are his tentacles showing?

What?

Oh, that was a little joke. Don't mind that. No, no. Nutso is very cute.

For a squirrel.

What? No, we don't have anything against squirrels.

(Fucking rodents)

They're adorable. Really, they are.

It's okay. Calm down.

Maybe you should check the doors and windows again. But only if Nutso says it is okay to do so. That's right. Make sure it's all okay with Nutso. Listen to your squirrel friend. He knows what is best for you. He knows what is best for all of us.

That's right. The Squirrel God knows best.
Go to A-25.

This is totally a trap.
Go to A-27.

A-24

Don't think we don't see the air quotes you're putting around that word.

It's okay. Don't fret about anything. We were merely attempting to get a baseline reading on your mental state before we started this psychological assessment. We've finished that initial investigation. You can go right ahead and start the therapy session with Dr. Nebuchenezzar now.

No, no. This won't count against you. It's quite all right. Remain calm.

Go to Section C. When prompted, please select C-2.

A-25

"Squirrel God," eh? Do you offer sacrifices to Squirrel God—we mean, "Nutso."

Oh, you wouldn't call them sacrifices. Okay, okay. What do you call them?

"Offerings."
Go to A-24.

"Nuts."
Go to A-26.

A-26

Wow. I don't think we've ever heard human sacrifices referred to as "nuts" before. We'll have to add that to the official lexicon.

So, is there any concrete correlation? Like, are you referring to a specific part of the human body when you talk about "nuts," or is it a general term that encompasses a whole range of body parts?

"Nuts" are testicles.
Go to A-43.

This is all a joke. You were kidding about the whole Squirrel God thing.
Go to A-45.

A-27

You are absolutely correct that this is a trap. What are you going to do about it? You have admitted to being under the influence of a trans-dimensional entity that manifests in your brain as a talking squirrel. Can you see how this might concern Asset Resource Management?

During Orientation & Inoculation, the Old Man told you that the Night Office was both Mother and Father. You swore to serve no gods other than the ones vetted by LOBE. You pledged that you would forswear all family, all friends, and all lovers. You took a blood oath to protect humanity from its own darkest nightmares. In return, the Night Office would take care of you—body and soul, mind and spirit.

And yet, you're still talking to an imaginary squirrel.

He's talking to you right now, isn't he? What's he saying?

Oh, the knife?

We haven't said anything about knives.

Have you looked ahead? You shouldn't do that. Peeking imperils the integrity of assessments like this. It's almost . . . cheating.

You're not a cheater, are you?

Whatever it takes to finish the mission.
Go to A-29.

Cheating isn't fair.
Go to A-31.

A-28

No imaginary friends? Is that what you are claiming now? But a minute ago, you said you had several, and that you used to light them on fire for fun. Which is it?

You were talking about plastic dolls.
Go to A-6.

You misunderstood the question, and would like to get on with the main part of the assessment now.
Go to A-30.

A-29

That's true. A Night Office field operative is expected to do whatever it takes to complete their mission. That is why Asset Resource Management gives field operatives a great deal of autonomy when they are in the field. You don't always have time to call in and get permission from Management.

But using the Way—looking ahead through time and space— is expressly forbidden unless you are a Guide. According to our records, you were the Closer on this last field operation.

In fact, there's a citation in your LIES that says LOBE has expressly forbidden you to undertake any Guide training. You aren't allowed to look into the Way.

No, we can't tell you why. LOBE's citation is sealed.

Don't be curious. We lose too many good field operatives every year to curiosity.

In fact, we should get on with the psychological assessment.

Go to Section C. When prompted, please select C-3.

A-30

What's the rush? Do you have another appointment? Do these questions make you nervous? Are you afraid of failing?

Yes. No. All of the Above.
Go to A-37.

Oh, this is bullshit? Okay, fine. You want to get started on the assessment. You're done talking about imaginary friends. Fine. Fine. We'll do that.
Go to A-39.

A-31

Were you paying attention that day during Orientation & Inoculation when the Old Man said that life wasn't fair? You must not have been. Were you daydreaming? Having a chat with your imaginary squirrel friend?

What was his name again?

"Nutso."
Go to A-32.

He doesn't have a name. You were lying about that earlier.
Go to A-34.

A-32

"Nutso"? That's a fine name for an imaginary squirrel. What does he eat?

"Nuts"
Go to A-43.

"Human flesh."
Go to A-44.

A-33

How did that feel? To drift apart from an imaginary friend? Did they not grow with you? Did someone tell you that it was time to put aside the things of childhood? Or did chatting with a talking squirrel fall out of vogue?

Well, it doesn't really matter. Imaginary friends can be like real friends, in this regard. Sometimes you do drift apart. There's no real reason. The two of you merely wake up one day and realize you haven't spoken in some time. It isn't anyone's fault. Not specifically. It's just . . . time. It happens.

It's a little sad, however, because this friend was perfect for you. Who do you have now?

Don't you feel a little regret about this? Late at night, when you are alone in bed, waiting for sleep to come. Knowing that it won't. Not tonight. The night would be less empty if you had a friend. Someone to pass the time with. Someone to make you feel . . . something.

Oh well. Perhaps we should start the assessment now.

Go to Section C.

A-34

Wow. Dig this hole a little deeper, why don't you?

Look, there's no reason to be defensive about this. Well, okay, there are a couple of reasons to be worried, but it's okay to be paranoid. That's part of what keeps you alive during field operations, isn't it? This healthy distrust of everything around you, especially those who say they mean to help.

When you are out in the field, no one is going to help you. Any entity that offers assistance has an ulterior motive, and that is not always to your benefit.

Which is why we are here, after all. We want to be sure that you didn't accept "assistance" from a third party while you were out.

You didn't, did you?

Okay, okay. We're just asking. It's easier for everyone if you are honest with us earlier than later. Right now, everything can be considered as an innocent mistake. The sort of gaffe a rookie makes—

No, we know this isn't your first mission. We weren't overlooking your service to the Night Office. No, no. We wouldn't do that. We know quite well how many times you've saved the universe. Three times, right?

That's right.
Go to A-36.

Actually, it's more like . . .
Go to A-38.

A-35

Is it painful to talk about the death of your imaginary squirrel friend?

It's okay. We understand. We don't need to know any details.

We are sorry for your loss.

Perhaps we should start the assessment now.

Your therapist's name is Dr. Nebuchenezzar. You can call him Dr. Nebs. He's going to ask you some questions about your recent field operation. He might ask you some questions about other people in your life as well, in an effort to formulate a complete psychic profile of you. It is best if you are honest with him—in fact, you will be completely honest with him, because he only exists in your head. You can't lie to yourself.

Yes, we know that's a lie. It's okay. It'll be our little secret. Shhh.

Go to Section C.

A-36

You are a valuable asset to this organization. We're not trying to trap you. This is a very straight-forward assessment. All you have to do is talk to your therapist for awhile. His name is Dr. Nebuchenezzar, though many folks call him "Dr. Nebs. He's waiting for you right now, in fact. While we've been talking about imaginary friends, your brain has been constructing the virtual therapy session. There were subliminal markers several pages back that started that process. It's okay. We didn't ask your subconscious to do anything it wasn't already primed to do so.

Remember that session about neuro-linguistic programming and auto-suggestion during Orientation & Inoculation? Oh, you don't remember that session. Perfect. Then everything worked like it was supposed to.

And yes, here we are. Are you ready to begin your session with Dr. Nebs?

Go to Section C.

A-37

It's hard to know who to trust, isn't it? When you are in the field, there are only three of you: the Opener, the Guide, and the Closer. You trust your team. Everyone else can fuck right off, especially once the Guide starts touching the Way. They are all trusting you to Close. The doors must be sealed. The portals must be shut down. The channels between here and there must be blocked. It's all on you.

Closing is not for the weak, is it? Your Opener can get eaten by one of the Black Goats of the Wood. Your Guide can get lost in the Way. But the Closer? The Closer has to hold their shit together and stand firm.

In the end, the only one you can really—truly—trust is yourself, right?

Makes it hard when you're not sure about yourself, doesn't it?

This is why we do this assessment after a field operation. We want to be sure that your personality is still intact. If you've been co-opted by space jellies, or if Txuexuan the Blender of Brains has dipped a talon in your gray matter and scrambled a lobe, we need to know.

It's okay to have doubts. We all do. But keep these moments of indecisiveness to when you're trying to decide between menu items at a fast food restaurant. Don't be like this in the field.

We clear?

Right. Let's get on with the rest of this assessment.
Go to Section C.

A-38

Five times? You've saved the universe five times already? Wow. Are you sure? Let's double-check this list. No, no. We're sure you're right. Our records must be wrong.

Let's see . . . there was the job in Pennsylvania. That was your first, right? And then there was the job in Albuquerque. Yes. That job. Oh, we all remember that job. So much clean-up. And then there was the job in Tennessee. The truck stop. Ah, yes. The truck stop. And then, that house in Boston, that one where—well, it's all in the report. We don't need to go over that again.

Shame what happened there.

What? Oh, that's only four. What's was the fifth job?

That was the job which the Old Man swore you to secrecy.
Go to A-47.

That was the job where . . . actually, you're not sure you're allowed to talk about it.
Go to A-48.

A-39

The assessment will start in a moment. We're just about ready. Please sit on that chair over there. Yes, the blue one. By the fish tank. Watch the fish swim for a few minutes while we finish texturing your therapist's office.

His name? Oh, it's Dr. Nebuchenezzar. Dr. Nebs, for short. You'll like him. He smokes a pipe. We're sure the scent of his tobacco will be soothing. Perhaps it will remind you of that ole auto-da-fé aroma . . .

Oh, did that trigger some kind of involuntary response? We apologize for that. Please sit down. There's no need to panic. Nothing's on fire . . .

Please. Sit down. Take some deep breaths. We want you to succeed in this assessment. We want to you be back out in the field as soon as possible. Yes, there are many monsters that need killing. Many incursions that need closing. You are a valuable asset to the Night Office. We do want you back in rotation as soon as possible.

Ah, there we go. Your session is ready.

Go to Section C. When prompted, please select C-2.

A-40

It's important that an Operation Assessment & Review (LIMB—OAR—12/r) is filed with Library Information Management Bureau after every field operation. We need to be able to catalog the team's field experience so that we keep up to date with the tactics and apprehensions of the vast variety of extra-terrestrial intelligences (and non-intelligences) that want to invade this planet. Your field operation may have been boring, but there could be some minor detail in your experience that LIMB and LOBE could use. They are always on the lookout for new defensive opportunities that could save all of humanity.

This is why you do paperwork, for crying out loud. Not because we're fixated on the minutia of the Universe.

Anyway, you should file that report, and when you have done so, come back and start this assessment again.

You may **skip to Section C** at that time.

A-41

Well, you won't be the first Night Office employee who "neglected" something on their Introspective Summary & Isolated Schematization form (PALM—ISS—33/r). It's a living document, much like your Life Integrity Experience Schematic. Topical Human Utilization Management & Benefits reviews all of this documentation on a regular basis. They will notice the holes—they always do. At that time, they'll ask you to fill out an Confessions & Self Advocation report (THUMB—CSA—43/d).

Don't worry. The garnishment of pay is only temporary. As a deterrent, of course. Not because THUMB bills ARM, much to the annoyance of EAR.

Go to Section C.

A-42

Indeed. Our question about space jelly goo is, in fact, another trap. Good job spotting it!

Last week, a field operative taking this assessment thought we were being friendly when we were talking about space jelly goo. They started talking about how hard it was to get out of pleather. We let them rattle on for awhile. It was a useful opportunity to observe how skillfully a space jelly can inject itself into a human brain. How much of the host can be flushed out before we notice that a person has been subjugated by an alien intelligence? The answer is: about 18%.

Anyway, once we were sure that this field operative had been co-opted by a Shoggoth, we dropped a thermal cone over them and torched them to ash. Didn't take long.

But you—you saw that we were testing you, and you didn't fall for it. Excellent work. You're ready for the next portion of this assessment.

Go to Section C.

A-43

Oh, wow. That's, uh, that's pretty gruesome. How often do you feed "nuts" to the Squirrel God?

Actually, never mind. We don't need to know.

Yeouch.

Okay, well—*technically*—this isn't in violation of your Personal Invocation & Promissory Exhortation contract (PALM—PIPE—87/es). It's a little . . . weird, but as long as it isn't getting in the way of your ability to execute your duties as a Closer, we'll overlook it.

However, if any sort of religious exercises or invocations involve other Night Office employees—either as willing participants or "accidental" contributors—we will have to report these infractions to the Human Asset Naturalization Department.

Well. We're glad we could have this talk. How about we get to that psychological assessment now?

Go to Section C. When prompted, please select C-3.

A-44

Oh, you feed human flesh to your imaginary friend? Wow. Well, we have a lot of follow-up questions. How often? How much? Where do you get it? Is it fresh?

Hold on. We're getting sidetracked. There's a form for this. Let's fill that form out first before we go any farther. Would you want a minute, please?

REPRESENTATIVES FROM THE HUMAN ASSET NATURALIZA- TION DEPARTMENT ON THEIR WAY. THEY ONLY FILL OUT FORMS AFTER THEY'VE SECURED A THREAT. JUST SO YOU KNOW...

MAPS SCORE: 4

A-45

Oh, there is no Squirrel God? It was all a joke. Okay, very funny. Ha ha. We're sure your teammates appreciated your sense of humor as well. It's a rare quality in a Night Office field operative. Perhaps you should consider signing up for the monthly talent show. There are cash prizes.

Go to Section C. When prompted, please select C-3.

A-46

Wait. What was that? There's a way to open the—?

THIS RESPONSE IS A TRAP.

IF YOU BELIEVE YOU ARE SUPPOSED TO BE READING THIS, YOU HAVE BEEN LED HERE BY A SUBLIMINAL DIRECTIVE. THAT MEANS SOMEONE IS TELLING YOU WHAT TO DO.

YOUR MIND IS NOT YOUR OWN. PLEASE CONFESS YOUR LACK OF SELF-CONTROL TO AN ADMINISTRATIVE AGENT.

MAPS SCORE: -5

BEYOND THE WALLS OF SANITY

A-47

Are you still talking to the Old Man? Is that . . . healthy?

He's been dead for awhile now, hasn't he? You were cleared of any wrongdoings in his death. We understand that he meant a lot to you. His betrayal hurt all of us. And he did a lot of good for the organization. We're not trying to excise him from the record, but . . . you know the ruling. We cannot speak of him. His presence has been excised from the records. It is best—for everyone.

You can't hang on to him. There are some within the organization that will see such nostalgia—such familiarity—as weakness. As a sign of corruption. They will want to watch you more closely. They won't trust you.

Believe us when we tell you that you don't want the Night Office wondering if you're playing for the right team.

Let him go. It's best for everyone. Find a new imaginary friend.

Maybe you shouldn't take this assessment. It's only going to get worse if you let them in. What else are they going to find?

You can't keep running . . .

Oh, you'll be careful? Oh, sure. We believe you.

Go to Section C. When prompted, please select C-2.

A-48

Oh, come on. You can totally fess up to it here. You do important work for the Night Office. You have to take a little pride in your work. How many times a week do we save the universe? A dozen? Two dozen? A lot, right?

It's not healthy to subsume these feelings of accomplishment. You can't bottle this up. You need to talk to someone now and again. In fact, that's what this therapy session is all about. Giving you an opportunity to talk to someone about what really goes on during a Night Office field operation. It will help. Honest. Tell your therapist everything. Don't hold anything back. It's the best way to ensure that we know what's going on in your head. It's the best way we can be sure that you can be trusted.

Okay?

Are you ready?

Go to Section C. When prompted, please select C-3.

SECTION B

ROLE-PLAYING

This section has been removed as
per HAND Direction 43/2/ae. Please
disregard any instructions for
SECTION B material and proceed to
Section C.

SECTION C

THERAPY

INITIALIZATION

During field operations, various extra-terrestrial intelligences may attempt to influence you, thereby altering your perception of objective reality. Your Guide may also be swayed by the Way, further warping perception of time and space. This may create psychological tension and neurological distress that may interfere with your ability to Close.

The realization of therapeutic personalities will help ground you in a subjective reality state that has existential ties to a more formalized objective reality. This assessment relies on a technique of self-generated therapeutic personalities, which can be used to extrapolate your psychological integrity.

You may retain the therapeutic personality generated by this assessment for use in the field, if such a personality is conducive to anchoring your self against psychic assault. This therapeutic personality is based on the psychoanalyst archetype. Your initial introduction to this personality will be through a visualized "therapy session." Please interact with this personality as you would an actual therapist.

If you are partial to the metaphorical investigations as found within the work of Carl Gustav Jung, **go to C-1.**

If you wish for this personality to be based on the classic psychoanalytic style of Sigmund Freud, **go to C-2.**

If you find the concept of armchair psychoanalysis off-putting and would rather have a therapeutic personality that is grounded in useful real-world methodologies, **go to C-3.**

Otherwise—or if you have been here before—**go to C-4.**

C-1

Dr. Nebuchenezzar's office is three blocks away from the Night Office. It's overcast today, and it's supposed to rain later. The wind is off the lake, and it smells fresh. When Dr. Nebs asks you how you are feeling, you think about that three block walk and you tell him that you're feeling pretty good.

"How are you sleeping?" he asks.

"Fairly well," you reply.

"Any difference since your last mission?"

He has a leather notebook that he writes in, and he always takes a few minutes to write some initial notes after he asks his first question. Just to give you some time to collect yourself. To give you the illusion that he isn't aware of your reaction to his question.

"I'm sleeping fine," you say. He smiles a little and finishes writing a note. You know he's writing down that you just lied to him. *This is how the patient is going to present themselves today,* is what he is writing.

He's too professional to just write "LIAR" in big letters.

That little smile means he's going to ask you again later, and he won't mind if you change your answer. As long as you pretend that you've come to a deep decision to change your ways with him. This is the game the two of you play, and it's been a long game, indeed.

"Have you experienced any traumatic shifts in perception since our last visit?" he asks.

"Like what?"

"Like being out of place in your own story. Are you worried that you might have missed something important?"

"I don't know, Doctor. Isn't that the very definition of life: always wondering if you've missed something?"

"Are you missing something?"

"No, Doctor. I'm fine."

"Very well," he says, making notes in his book.

You try to get comfortable on his couch. It's a nice couch, and you should be able to relax, but you can't quite seem to find a good position. You know he is watching you squirm.

"How was your last mission?" he asks.

"It was fine," you reply.
Go to C-5.

"It could have gone better," you reply.
Go to C-7.

C-2

Dr. Nebuchenezzar's office is located downtown. You take a cab, and traffic is heavy enough that the drive takes twenty minutes longer than you anticipated. You are now late for your appointment. You throw money at the cab driver, tell him to keep the change (which wasn't much, frankly), and you hurry into the building.

Dr. Nebuchenezzar's office is on the third floor. You don't wait for the elevator, and you hustle up the three flights of stairs. There are several other people in the waiting room; you don't recognize any of them (thank God). You check in with the receptionist; she gives you a bit of a stink-eye about being late. "It will be a few minutes," she says. "We'll call you when it is time."

You go sit in the corner. There are magazines on the table. You pick one up and leaf through it without really paying attention to any of the pictures. You try not to draw attention to yourself.

In about a half hour, the receptionist looks up from her desk and says, "Dr. Nebuchenezzar will see you now."

You go to the inner door, which the receptionist unlocks for you. On the other side, you find a narrow hall that ends in an another door. You go through this door

(so many doors)

and find yourself in a neatly furnished office. Walnut bookcases line one wall. A large picture window looks out over the city. A leather couch is placed beneath this window. Opposite the couch is a leather chair, and standing beside the chair is a tall man in a tight suit. His hair is neatly combed, and the ends of his tidy mustache are waxed. It makes him look like he is perpetually smiling.

It's a little off-putting, actually.

Anyway, he offers his hand and introduces himself. You are supposed to be on good behavior here, so you return the greeting. He doesn't hold your hand long.

"Please, sit down," he says, indicating the couch under the window.

You sit. He folds himself into his chair and opens a leather notebook. He is using an ornate pen, and when he writes, you can hear the nib scratching on the paper.

"How are you feeling today?" he asks.

"Fine," you say.

"Is that all?"

"Yeah," you say. "That's all."

"Pity," he says.

"What do you mean?"

"It means we have some work ahead of us," he says. "What should we talk about first? Your suppressed rage about your mother or your disappointment about your father?"

"This seems a little abrupt," you say.

He shrugs. "It's your mind," he notes. "I didn't see any point in beating around the bush."

"Okay, fine. Let's talk about my mother."
Go to C-11.

"Yeah, okay. Fair point. Let's talk about dad."
Go to C-13.

C-3

Dr. Nebuchenezzar's office is located in the building across the street from the Night Office. Traffic is heavy enough that you go to the corner and wait for the light. As you waiting for the light, a dirty man wearing a sports team jersey approaches you and asks if you have any change. You tell him to go away, and when the light changes, you find yourself walking quickly across the street.

You keep checking over your shoulder as you walk to the building where Dr. Nebs's office is located.

Inside, the elevator is out of service, and you have to take the stars. You are out of breath when you reach the fourth floor. In the lobby here, there is no sign on the elevator about it being out of service.

You knock on the door to Dr. Nebs's office. After a moment, the lock buzzes and you can go in. You wander through an empty waiting area, and then through another door into Dr. Nebs's office.

He's a thin man who likes to wear a sweater under his suit jacket. "How are you feeling today?" he asks as he indicates you should sit on the couch near the window.

"I'm fine," you reply.

You can see the sidewalk in front of the building from this window. You wonder if the man in the dirty sports jersey followed you. You could check.

Yes, you should definitely check.
Go to C-6.

No, don't check.
Go to C-8.

C-4

Sanity is so overrated, isn't it? Especially in the Night Office. They tell you this in the first week of training: one of you will have a nervous breakdown before you finish training, two of you will start manifesting significant psychological distress within three months, four of you will develop self-destructive tendencies as coping mechanisms, six of you will have reoccurring nightmares, and the rest of the you will start drinking heavily. Most of the class laughs—there are only fourteen of you, after all.

If anything, the statistics have been seriously sugar-coated.

What they don't tell you is only ten percent of any given training group will demonstrate the aptitude necessary for field operatives, and of that fraction, only one in six will be suitable for Closing. Which is a problem, because what is the primary goal of the Night Office? That's right: closing doors.

The average life expectancy of a Closer is eighteen months, plus or minus six weeks, depending on how many assignments you get called out for. Management rotates Closers off the roll after twenty-four months, putting them in front of students for a year while they are monitored for psychic cracks. Most don't pass re-certification.

All of which is to say that rigorous self-care and persistent mental self-examination are a critical part to job success as a Night Office Closer. While Management doesn't encourage invention of fictitious psychological constructs as a means of psychic armor against the dangers of your job, they don't actively discourage it either. Many Closers fabricate some sort of imaginary world as a coping mechanism.

It helps to have friends, and if you can't figure out how to make them in the real world, then the ones in your head will have to suffice.

At the very least, talk to your pets. That's what they are there for. They're pretty good listeners. Especially Mr. Fish.

Anyway, these invented personalities are distinct from your own consciousness, right? You're not schizophrenic, and you're not "hearing voices." You merely have a healthy mental organization that is conducive to instructive internal dialogue. It helps to have other world-views, as it were, that you can query when you are attempting to work out a thorny problem. There are times when the only reality you can trust is the subjective ground beneath your feet, so to speak.

All of this is self-justification for Dr. Nebs and these therapy sessions. He reminds you of Dalton Perth, the old guy who owned that bookstore Clarice used to take you to all the time when you were growing up. It was a safe place, wasn't it? And he always made you tea, with lots of milk. He was the one you talked to first when you started to realize you were different. That your aunt was different. That the world wasn't how you thought it was. And he listened, didn't he? He never judged. He would always make more tea or find you a book that—somehow—made things better.

You don't have to justify your internal world to anyone. Just as long as it keeps you sane.
Go to C-9.

But if you've invented your therapist, what else have you invented? How much of all this is just your own confusion, wrapping itself around you? Uh oh. Maybe you haven't gotten everything sorted out.
Go to C-10.

C-5

"Why don't you start at the beginning?" Dr. Nebs suggests. He turns to a new page in his notebook.

"We recently cleared a house," you say, figuring to stick with recent events.

"We?"

"Yeah, I was on a team."

"How did that go for you?"

"As well as you'd expect for a Night Office excursion."

Dr. Nebs knows better than to respond like your peers. *That bad, eh?* And then everyone would share a knowing laugh. No, Dr. Nebs is a professional. He merely nods and moves on. "Do you want to talk about it?" he asks.

"I suppose I'm expected to," you reply.

"Well, if I wanted to know what happened—officially—I could read the report, couldn't I?"

"Yeah, you could."

"But that's not why we are here," he says. He writes in his notebook. You suspect it's not anything important. He's merely drawing this out. Waiting to see your reaction. How well you react to silence. Are there things you didn't mention in the report that are eating at you. Do you feel guilt? Shame? How much are you hiding?

This is a trap, of course. The first of many, you expect. This exercise in lucid actualization is a clever mechanism whereby the Night Office sees if you can handle the stress of the job. Whether or not the guilt will devour you.

You are imagining all of this. The office. This couch. The therapy session. Even Dr. Nebs. He's just a mental construct that allows you to interrogate your own fractured psyche. Your own psychic armor is being tested. Are you strong enough?

"You're doubting yourself," Dr. Nebs says.

"Maybe," you say, echoing him from a moment earlier.

"Do you know what happens when we are finished with this session?"

"I don't know what happens," you say.
Go to C-16.

"You give me a grade. Like this is a spelling test or something."
Go to C-17.

C-6

You sit on the couch and lean toward the window. You pull the curtain aside and look down at the street in front of the building. Sure enough, you see the old man in the sports jersey. He's parked himself next to a trash container, and he is trying to catch the attention of people wandering by. Begging for spare change.

As you look, he spasms suddenly. Coins fly out of his cup. But instead of chasing after them, he raises his head, looking right at you.

You duck back, letting the curtain fall. Your heart is racing. He didn't see you, did he? You're not sure. How could he have known you were looking?

"Is everything all right?" Dr. Nebs asks.

"I'm fine," you say quickly.

After making a note, Dr. Nebs folds his hands and places them on his notebook. He stares at you. His eyes are gentle and compassionate. He seems like he really wants to understand what you are going through.

"I'm not going through anything," you say quickly. "I'm fine."

He presses his lips together, but doesn't say anything. He's giving you the silent treatment, almost as if he knows you are lying.

Of course he knows. He's a construct of your own imagination. He knows everything. What you did at the house. What you did during college. What got you thrown out of your aunt's house. All those things. As long as you remember them, he'll remember them.

"This wasn't the plan," you say.

"What plan?" Dr. Nebs asks.

The bastard knows, you think.

You turn around on the couch and look out the window again. The homeless guy is still down there. He knows too, doesn't he?

"Are you afraid that everyone knows?" Dr. Nebs asks.

"No," you say quickly.

"Are you sure?"

"Why don't we stick to the reason we are here," you say. "Aren't you supposed to debrief me or something?"

"Debrief you about what?"

"The last mission. Aren't you supposed to make sure I didn't lose my mind while fighting space jellies or something."

"Did you?"

"Did I what?"

"Fight space jellies."

"Maybe," you admit.

Dr. Nebs raises his eyebrow. "You don't remember?"

"It was dark. I was tired. It was raining."

"Is this the same excuse you used when you were accused of stealing Alison Cambrie's necklace?"

"Who?"
Go to C-25.

"What necklace?"
Go to C-28.

C-7

"How could the mission have gone better?" Dr. Nebs asks.

"Well, everyone else could have come home too," you say.

"True," Dr. Nebs admits. He makes a note in his book.

"What are you writing down?" you ask.

"Nothing important," he says.

"Yes, but every time you write, I think it is important. It makes me second-guess myself."

Dr. Nebs makes another note.

You try not to let his constant doodling get under your skin. It's what he's supposed to do, isn't it? Needle you until you make a mistake. Though, what do you have to hide, really?

"Yes," Dr. Nebs says quietly. "What are you hiding? You were the only survivor of your operation. Is the 'you' that came back the same 'you' that went out?"

"That's the question, isn't it? Have I been compromised by my experience?"

"Did you make contact with . . . anything?"

"I flashed a space jelly."

Dr. Nebs makes a note. "I'm putting a hash mark in your tally," he explains. "This was a good note."

"Right, right," you say. "How many is that now?"

"Eleven," he says. "Two more and you get a prize."

"I do?"

"Or maybe it is merely a raise." He taps his pen against his bottom lip. "I can never quite remember."

You think about what sort of prize you might like for killing a dozen—no, thirteen—space jellies. Sure, a raise would be nice, but what would you spend that money on? More food for—

"Oh, so you got a pet," Dr. Nebs says, picking up your stray thought.

"Why don't we talk about the mission," you say, getting back on track. "I'd rather talk about the mission."
Go to C-59.

"After flashing that jelly, I found something interesting," you say, redirecting the conversation.
Go to C-61.

C-8

If Dr. Nebuchenezzar notices your hesitation, he doesn't say anything.

"Make yourself comfortable," he says.

You sit on the couch.

He writes in his notebook for a moment. The pen is terribly noisy. You can almost feel the nib tearing at the paper. Like a fingernail, picking at a scab.

"How are you sleeping?" he asks.

"About the same," you say.

"That much?"

You shrug. "It's what my body needs," you say.

"Nothing to do with the medications you are taking?"

"I'm not taking any medications," you remind him.

"Not prescribed ones, at any rate."

You don't have an answer to that. Your drinking is within the allowances of your Night Office contract.

Dr. Nebs sighs theatrically. "I'm a therapeutic personality construct," he says. "I'm in your head. I know what you are thinking. You can't lie to me."

Yes, I can, you think.

It is his turn to stare. Eventually, he looks down at his notebook. His pen moves across the page. *Scritsch scritsch.* The noise is maddening.

You need a distraction. Think of something else.
Go to C-20.

No, not *that*. Think of something else.
Go to C-81.

C-9

"Excellent," Dr. Nebs says.

You start, and for a moment, you don't know where you are. Then, you recognize the pale ecru walls of the psychologist's office. The off-white painting that hangs on the wall at the foot of the patient couch. The one he tells you is a picture of a rabbit in a snowstorm. When you told him that Rothko never painted landscapes, he merely smiled.

"What the hell just happened?" you ask.

"It's a memory loop," Dr. Nebs says simply. "You're untethered from this reality. Your mind is trying to find its way back from the Dark Labyrinth."

"The what?"

He frowns as he consults his notebook. "Ah, you must think it is March."

"What?" You are so confused.

"March," he says again. "Before you found . . . " He trails off, and his frown deepens.

"How do I—how do I find my way out of this . . . this labyrinth?"

Dr. Nebs offers you a tiny smile. "I don't know, actually."

"Oh, lovely. And you're supposed to be helping me."

"We're all helping you," he says.

"Why?" You rewind his sentence. "And who?"

"The Night Office," he says. "Because we don't want you to destroy the world. Isn't that the way it always is?"

"It is," you admit. "Why am I going to destroy the world?"

"Because They told you to."

"They?"

He nods conspiratorially. "*They*."

"The terrors from another dimension."

"Yes," he admits.

"The abominations from another temporality."

He tilts his head. "Them too."

"The space refugees from that dead star in Andromeda."

He shakes his head. "The *Voerdamnikenari*? Not them."

"Oh, well, that's a relief," you say.

"Some of the Old Ones, however . . . "

"Of course." You look up at the ceiling fan. "It's not a party without Cth—"

He stops you with a loud cough. "We don't"—he smiles weakly—"we don't say that name here."

"Why not? He's not Hast—"

"*Zzziiittt!* Not that one either."

That's when it occurs to you: you're not afraid of invoking the names of the Old Ones. Why wouldn't you be afraid of drawing their attention? Is it because you know they won't come? Or is it because they are dead?

Or it is because you think you can defeat them?

"What—what did I do?" you ask. Your mouth is dry, and you suddenly yearn for a glass of water. Or whiskey. Whichever is handier.

"You know what you did," Dr. Nebs says.

"I'm going to destroy the world, aren't I?" you croak.

"Unless we can stop you," Dr. Nebs says. He leans forward in his chair. "You have to find your way out of the Labyrinth. It's the only way you can close these gaps in your mind. It's the only way to wind back what has been unwound."

"I have to find my way," you whisper. You look up at the white painting again. It reminds you of something.

"I need to close the gaps," you say.
Go to C-12.

"I'm not myself," you say.
Go to C-14.

C-10

On the eighth—or maybe it was the ninth—day of Night Office training, your instructor spent the morning talking about our objective lack of understanding about reality really works. The human mind—according to this instructor—is psychologically incapable of sustaining reality on its own. It—we—need the cooperation of other minds. *Reality "works"*—he air quotes that word very theatrically—*because we all agree that it does.* Left to your own devices—or thoughts, to be more precise—reality frays. We don't sustain the bits that don't feel relevant, but it's all relevant, isn't it? Especially when you're the one who is supposed to be holding it all together.

Who was it who said that we murder in the course of creating something? Was that Wordsworth? Trust a poet to slip a secret of the universe into a stanza about the way moss crawls up the side of a cathedral wall.

Anyway, the point here is that if you are cut off from the rest of humanity, reality is going to get slippery. While the Night Office likes to scoop up runaways, orphans, malcontents, and misanthropes, it does like everyone to be on the same page.

Are we leaning on the book metaphor too much? It'll get thicker later, don't worry.

The point here is that a support structure is useful. No, it's critical, because we have demonstrated—time and again—that a collection of tiny lights shine very brightly. All you need is—

Oh, wait. You're a loner. You've been on your own since those early school days, haven't you? Since Clarice said she didn't want anything to do with the woman you had become. Since she cast you out.

Go ahead. Call her a "bitch." You're not wrong. But blaming her for abandoning you is the wrong way to look at it. You wouldn't be in this place right now if she hadn't turned her back on you. But that argument places the responsibility of caring for you on her. It was her responsibility to ensure you had community (even though Dr. Nebs might argue that her idea of community was just the two of you, which wasn't "community" per se, but a dominant / submissive relationship).

When you're done feeling sorry for yourself, how about focusing on the Dark Labyrinth before your mind splinters into a hundred million pieces.

No one will be able to put that puzzle back together again.

Puzzles are the worst. Let's not end up like that, thank you very much.
Go to C-18.

This is all too weird. You don't have an aunt named Clarice. You don't believe in magic. And you certainly don't believe that you're the only one who can stop eldritch horrors from devouring humanity.
Go to C-15.

C-11

"What do you want to know about my mother?" you ask.

"What do you want to tell me?" Dr. Nebs replies.

"Is it going to be like that?"

He shrugs. "This can be as simple or as complicated as you want to make it," he says.

"I'd like it to be simple," you say.

"Talk simply," he says.

"Fuck you," is your reply.

He glances at his watch and then makes a note in his book. "Not ten minutes into the session," he says. "I think we're making progress."

"Progress on what?"

"Determining whether you are still human."

"Is that what this is all about?"

"Of course it is. Didn't you read the fine print?"

"I never read the fine print," you say.

He makes another note in his book. You try not to let it aggravate you. "Your mother . . . ?" he prompts.

"She left when I was very young," you say. "I don't remember much about her."

"Someone else, then. Who was the closest thing you had to a mother?"

"Clarice, I suppose. My aunt."

"And what was your relationship like with your aunt?"

"Before or after . . . ?"

He gives you a thin-lipped smile. "Before, of course. I know what happened after."

"It was fine," you say. "She did all the right things. Said all the right phrases that the schools wanted to hear. Made them the vague promises that all well-intentioned parents make."

"And you? Did you say the 'right things'?"

"I tried. Once or twice."

"Why didn't you try harder?"

You don't answer him. He waits for a minute, hoping you might change your mind, but you don't. You stare up at the ceiling while he writes in his book.

"Does your relationship with your mother—"

"My aunt."

"Your aunt, yes. Does you relationship with her have an impact on your ability to form relationships with other people?"

"In what way?"

"Trust, perhaps."

You try to keep the grimace off your face. "Maybe," is all you are willing to say.

"Did you have trouble trusting your team?"

He hesitate too long.

"Why didn't you trust them?" he asks.

You knew they were going to die. Why make friends if they aren't going to be around for very long?

Go to C-50.

"Trust is a two-way street," you say.

Go to C-76.

C-12

"I'm caught in a psychological feedback loop, aren't I?"

Dr. Nebs makes a 'pock-pock-pock' noise with his mouth. "It can happen during sessions like this," he says. "When a field operative suffers some sort of psychotic episode during a field operation, they may appear to be normal. They can talk. They can engage in conversation. But they are poised on an existential collapse. One that will separate them from the nominal flow of sensory experience and time. These sessions are meant to apply pressure to the field operative in a way that will exacerbate possible stressors."

"Stressors? You make it sound like I'm supposed to lose my mind."

"It is better for a field operative to have their psychotic break while they are somewhere . . . safe." He adjusts his pant leg. "Do you feel safe?"

"No," you say.

"Well, I guess we're going to have to work on that a bit more," he says. He pauses for a moment, and you realize you're supposed to laugh.

"I left my extra laughs back at the office," you say.

"Next to your box of fucks, I suppose."

"No, that box was empty."

"Of course."

"Can we get to the part where you tell me how to get out of these . . . whatever these are?"

"Neuro-existential quantum loops."

"Sure. Whatever. Those. How do I get out of them?"

"Well, you need to ground yourself. Not to what *is* true, but what you *need* to be true. Once you are comfortable with that, then you can begin to explore the rest of the conscious world around you. You can't be a subjective point in space until you have achieved some level of individual objectivity."

"I can't exist until I know I exist. Something like that?"

"Something like that."

"That's kind of subjective."

"All of reality is *kind of subjective*, so don't press too hard."

"Fair enough."

You lie on the couch for awhile, staring at the ceiling fan. Watching it go around and around. Dr. Nebs doesn't say anything, but you can hear his pen going *scritsch scritsch* on the paper.

"What are you writing?" you ask finally.

"I'm drawing," he says.

"What are you drawing?"

"A white rabbit in a snowstorm," he says.

Curious about how that works, you get up from the couch and walk over to where he is sitting. His pad is covered with scribbles, hashes, and blots. There's no pattern to it that you can discern. You certainly don't see a white rabbit.

"Of course not," Dr. Nebs says. "It's snowing."

"You've lost your mind," you say.

"Look who is talking," Dr. Nebs fires back.

Go to C-91.

"This isn't helping," you say.

"Whose fault is that?" Dr. Nebs asks.

Go to C-84.

C-13

"I don't know who my father was," you tell Dr. Nebs. "His name isn't on the birth certificate. My mom wasn't very—well, she left when I was three, so I don't have much recollection of anything she might have told me. And Clarice—"

"Clarice?" Dr. Nebs interrupts.

"My aunt."

"Ah. She's the one who raised you?"

"Basically."

"Was there a man in her life? Someone who might have been a surrogate father to you?"

You laugh. "Which one?"

Dr Nebs frowns. "I don't understand."

"Which of the—I don't know—dozen, two dozen men in Clarice's life should I designate as a surrogate father?"

"Were any of them kind to you?"

"Most of them were," you say. "But then, most of them also ignored me, so I suppose that qualifies as kindness too."

"I'm not sure it does," Dr. Nebs argues, albeit gently.

"It doesn't really matter now," you tell him. "None of them lasted very long."

"How does that make you feel?"

"You mean, is this what pushed me to liking women?"

He makes a vague gesture with his hand.

"Yes," you say. "No. Maybe. It doesn't matter. I think you'll be hard pressed to see correlation between my aunt and her relationships with an endless parade of dim-witted fools and my own predilections towards companionship."

"I wasn't suggesting there was a correlation."

"Good," you say. "Because that was a choice I made. It's not a reaction to what I saw going on around me."

"Very good," he says. He looks down and starts, as if he has just remembered that he is supposed to be taking notes. His pen scribbles for awhile before he asks his next question.

"How did you feel toward the men on your team?"
Go to C-77.

"Were there any women in your team?"
Go to C-78.

C-14

"Who else would you be?" Dr. Nebs asks.

"That's kind of why we are here, isn't it?"

He makes a vague gesture with his pen, indicating you should explain your question.

"This wasn't the first time I encountered a shoggoth, you know. There was that time in Ohio. We encountered four of them there. Our Opener took care of several of them before they ate his brain. I watched his eyes change, and then I blew his head off with a shotgun." You let out a short bark of laughter. "That was the worst thing I could have done, because shoggoths spatter. They make a mess, and the worst part is that they aren't dead. No, to kill a shoggoth, you have to destroy them utterly. Burn 'em. Freeze 'em. Or Close them. That's the best way. They're like weeds, you know. They always grow back."

"How do you feel about . . . disposing of that shoggoth?"

"Well, I lived. Other people didn't. The job got done. How I feel is sort of beside the point."

"It certainly isn't," Dr. Nebs says. "It leaves a mark on you. We're here to assess whether that mark is temporary or . . . ?"

"Or what?"

"Has your experience changed you?"

"I'm fine," you say.
Go to C-63.

"It's nothing," you insist. "I could kill shoggoths all day long without suffering any 'psychological trauma.' They're space jellies. It's my job."
Go to C-71.

C-15

Seriously? You're just going to stick your head in the sand and pretend that the universe isn't a vast and empty place where the only other intelligences that we are ever going to bump into are so indifferent to us that we might as well be dust?

Well, okay. Fine. Go off and join the great majority of humanity who are going to sleep, fuck, and panic their way through their miserable and pointless lives. Maybe if you sleep, fuck, and panic better than the rest of them, they might give you a shiny medal or something. They can bury you with it when you are dead. That'll be satisfying, right?

Sure. Whatever. Get me the fuck out of this.
Go to C-65.

Hang on. On second thought, that sounds terrible. Maybe you should try this again.
Go to C-5.

C-16

Dr. Neb makes a notation in his book. "Well, after we get done here, you will confront the Dark Labyrinth."

"The what?"

"The Dark Labyrinth," he says. "It is what every field operative faces after they have confronted some manner of eldritch insanity. Surely this was mentioned in your briefings?"

"I must have been . . . thinking of other things," you say.

Dr. Nebs frowns. "Do you know about the egress?" he asks. He scribbles in his notebook. The sound his pen makes on the paper is starting to annoy you. It sounds like something scrabbling at a wall.

"What is the . . . the egress?"

"The way out."

"Why would I need to find that?" you ask. "What are you talking about?"

Dr. Neb makes a dismissive motion with his lips as he continues to write.

You can't look at him any more. You turn away and discover the windows have been covered with heavy curtains. "When—when did you put those in?" you ask. This is confusing. The curtains weren't here last time. In fact, they weren't here a moment ago . . .

(are you sure?)

"A week ago," Dr. Neb says. "Tuesday afternoon, I think."

"Why?"

He looks up from his notes. "Do you dislike them?" he asks. "Do they make this environment seem more . . . constrictive?"

"Yes," you say.

"Good," he says. "That's an honest answer. Now we're getting somewhere."

You don't like not being able to see the world outside this office. It makes you wonder if it still exists.

"We were talking about your condition . . ." Dr. Neb prompts.

"I'm fine," you answer reflexively.

"You're not," he counters. "You wouldn't be here otherwise."

"I . . . I just wanted to check in," you say.

"How deep in the Labyrinth are you?" he asks suddenly.

"I'm not," you insist. "I don't even know what the Labyrinth is."
Go to C-75.

"I . . . Am I? Maybe." This is getting confusing. Better to admit it now. "I think I am lost," you say.
Go to C-73.

C-17

"A grade?" Dr. Nebs makes a pouting shape with his lips. "I don't give you a grade. Your actions generate a psychological matrix that is assessed by PINEAL—"

"Who?"

"Psychological Investment Notary & Emotional Analysis Legation," he says. "An aspect of the Night Office."

"Oh, of course," you say. It is hard to keep up with all the various departments within the organization. Sometimes it feels overly byzantine by design and not by bureaucratic accident.

"PINEAL will assign you a MAPS score—"

You're pretty sure you should know this acronym, but it escapes you at the moment.

"—which corresponds to how deep you are in the Dark Labyrinth, which is—"

"Wait a minute. The what?"

"The Dark Labyrinth."

"What is that?"

Dr. Nebs sighs. "You were daydreaming, weren't you?"

"No," you lie. "I was trying to remember an acronym."

"Pay attention. This is very important."

"Okay, okay. I'll pay attention." You make a show of settling into the couch.

"The Dark Labyrinth is a psychological construct," Dr. Neb says. "It was invented—well, it was discovered, rather—during the period of experimentation that followed the Second World War. Stanford. MK-ULTRA. Operation Blue Book. Things the Russians were doing."

"I thought Blue Book was about UFOs," you interject.

Dr. Neb stares at you for a second over the rim of his glasses. You offer him a weak smile and wave a hand for him to continue.

"Under certain inducements, patients could be convinced that they would be capable of withstanding varying degrees of psychic assault. They were taught to build a tessellating labyrinth that invaders had to navigate in order to gain access. Sort of a higher order version of the psychic defenses Fortune taught the British Occult Corps during the early part of the twentieth century."

You nod, having vague recollections of hearing about this during one of those tedious lectures classes you had to sit through during the second year of Night Office training.

"However, it was after the Incarnate Excursion that it became clear that these constructs were, in fact, opening rituals."

"Opening rituals? Like, in your mind?"

Dr. Nebs nods. "Yes. By invoking the Dark Labyrinth, you allow space jellies access to your brain."

"Wait. What? I thought I was supposed to keep space jellies out of my head?"

Dr. Nebs frowns. "Who told you that?"

"Everyone told me that. We're reminded every day during Orientation & Inoculation."

"Well, that is unfortunately out of date information."

"I think you're wrong," you say.
Go to C-66.

Dr. Nebs has to be lying. But can he? He's an invented therapeutic personality. If he is lying, that means you're lying to yourself. Does that mean you're not yourself? Were you co-opted by a space jelly during that last mission?

There's only one way to find out.

You jump up from the couch, and before Dr. Neb can stop you, you run for the door. You yank it open, hoping to catch some part of your brain off-guard. If you can leap into another memory, perhaps you can find a crack you can exploit . . .
Go to C-20.

C-18

Hold on. You're getting ahead of yourself. There is no Dark Labyrinth. Not yet, anyway. There's just the matter of having a support network to help out when you are trying to save the Universe from being turned inside out. Remember what they taught you. Start from the beginning, which was . . .

Nothingness, right?

No, that's not it. It's *something*. Not the Void—we definitely don't start with that. Start with the Alpha. The first thing. The first principle. The individuation of God, as it were. Whatever works. Just remember this. In the beginning, there is *something*.

Then, that something perceives something else. In Christian mythology, this is when God separates the light from the dark. (Somewhat heavy-handedly, of course, but always play to the cheap seats in the back, right?) And everything was groovy. Now you have *one* thing and *another* thing. Quantifiably, you can now distinguish what is and what is not. You can't have subjectivity until you have objectivity. And vice versa.

You're making progress. One step at a time. One thing at a time. From this comes all the rest.

This is how you keep your sanity.

There you go. Take a deep breath. Remember how you got here. Remember there is always a way *through*.

There is rarely a way back.

Focus on something else. That'll help ground you.
Go to C-20.

You're still not convinced this isn't all a game of smoke and mirrors.
Go to C-19.

C-19

Of course it is all smoke and mirrors. Perception is subjective. Reality doesn't care what you think of it. And there will always be monsters. Stop sniveling, and get back to work.

You feel properly chastised.
Go to Section C. Please choose a different therapeutic personality model.

You are starting to wonder if this is all lies. Every bit of it. There's something else at work here, isn't there? Something more insidious.
Go to C-22.

C-20

Here we go, this memory will be innocuous. Dr. Nebuchenez-zar won't find anything amiss with this.

Two weeks into Orientation & Inoculation, you had an encounter with a man from THUMB—Topical Human Utilization Management & Benefits. His name was Gerlacher, and he came looking for you. Apparently there was a document that you hadn't filled out before starting Orientation & Inoculation.

Anyway, Gerlacher looked like someone stuffed a lobster in a wool suit and glued a blond wig on his head. He breathed heavily through his nostrils, and he snapped at the ends of his words like an anxious dog. Thankfully, he didn't have much to say.

"Read it," he said of the two-page document on the table. "Initial in the marked spots."

What was it called? Oh, yes, that was the PALM—WRI—54/q. The Willing & Ready Invocation form.

You looked at the document. You read it over. Twice. Eventually, you confessed that you hadn't thought to bring a pen to this meeting. He stared at you for a moment before he opened open one of the drawers of the desk and rooted around. You heard a lot of metal clattering against metal, and then he slapped an object down on the desk.

It was a metal case with a small stud at one end. When you pressed it, a small blade flicked out.

"What the hell?"

"You didn't bring a pen." Gerlacher spread his large hands, and you noticed the tips of his fingers are stained. *How long has he been working in this department?* you wondered. Stabbing his fingers day in and day out. "You can leave if you want," he said. "But you go no further without signing this."

You idly held the stud down on the switchblade and pressed the tip of the knife into the desk. The blade slide back into the case. You pushed the stud, and the blade flicked out again.

To distract that cunning part of your mind from this . . . toy, you read the document a second time.

The PALM—WRI—54/q was fairly mundane in its language, but rather unique in its subject matter. The first disclaimer you had to initialize stated that you were fully aware of the psychological torment that came with the job. You would, the disclaimer implied, very likely go insane at some point during your tenure as a Night Office field operative. There was a second spot to initial where you acknowledged that you would not hold the Night Office responsible for trauma—mental, physical, emotional, spiritual, and/or metaphysical—associated with any horrors you might be exposed to. Furthermore (third spot to initial) you acknowledged that most of humanity wasn't capable of understanding the sacrifices you might be required to make in order to save the world.

In return, the Night Office offered a life insurance policy that would be paid regardless of the manner of your death. The Night Office didn't care how you died. Implied in there wasn't an "if" but a "when." *When* you died, they would pay a lump sump to the charity of your choice.

Last spot to initial: *the Night Office will not acknowledge any claims, legal action, or appeals to the common good made by friends, relatives, kin, dependents, or members of a community organization that might have selected you as some sort of motivational mascot or martyr.*

All of which was to say, if you had to take matters into your own hands in order to save the universe, the Night Office would honor your self-sacrifice accordingly. But they would never admit to what you had to do, or that you did it for them.

You pressed the tip of the blade against the wide part of your thumb. When a dot of blood appeared, you daubed it on the document—*there, there, there,* and *there.* Then you pricked your index finger and scrawled something that looked like your signature across the bottom of the second page.

That was all Gerlacher needed. He reached into his jacket and brought out a wide-bladed gravity knife. He flicked it open, sliced his thumb, and put his thumbprint on the page. His blood was darker than yours, and it dried quickly.

Gerlacher cleaned his blade with a small piece of silk. Both the silk and the knife went back into his jacket. "What charity would you like to honor?" he asked.

"Humane Society," you responded. The cats and dogs of the world were worth saving. Everything else . . .

He heaved himself out of his chair and left the room.

(no, that's not how it happened)

Look. He forgot the switchblade . . .

If you picked it up, **go to C-21**.

If you left without taking it, **go to C-23**.

C-21

Knives are dangerous, especially in hands like yours.

You can almost here Dr. Nebuchenezzar saying this. He isn't, though. You're remembering this. He wasn't there, when Gerlacher came to you about the PALM—WRI—54/q form. The good doctor wasn't even a figment of your imagination then.

He's more than a figment now, you think. Watching you. Knowing your every thought.

Do you remember Marylynn Velasquez? Dr. Nebuchenezzar asks suddenly. He's so close; it's like he is in your head. *You thought you could trust her. You thought she wanted the same thing you did. And it turned out that what she really wanted was to talk you into doing a threesome with Larry Tollisson.*

As if Larry would respect her more afterward, you think. *What a stupid girl.*

When you said no—because: *ew,* right?—she told stories about you. Word got around. Rumors started. People started to stare. Some even talked behind your back, whispering amongst themselves. Thinking you couldn't hear them.

But you could, didn't you? That was one of the first tricks you learned.

And Marylynn? Fortunately, her daddy was a plastic surgeon. He fixed the scars on the outside, but he couldn't do anything about the ones on the inside. She hid them from him, of course, desperate to be a dutiful and respectful daughter. Oh, but you you and everyone else knew otherwise, didn't you?

It's been a long time since you'd held a knife like this. *Knives are always useful later,* you told yourself.

As if you needed an excuse, Dr. Nebuchenezzar writes in his notebook.

You don't see his note until later, but he's writing it now, his pen going *scritsch scritsch*.

You turn away from the table—the one in your memory, the one that is almost more real now than the therapist's office—and approach the door. It's a plain door. Off-white. It looks like it came off an assembly line that spits out a couple hundred doors an hour. *How many doors could a factory make in a year?* you wonder. In ten years? Forget unexplored places on maps. Doors will connect every place anyone could ever want to go. You'll never be lost again.

That's a joke, by the way. There will always be a way to get lost. Like now, for instance. Given the way your brain is fragmenting.

Where were you going? Oh, yes, back to Dr. Nebuchenezzar's. There's unfinished business to attend to.
Go to C-24.

There's something you need to do, isn't there? No, not *that*. That will come later. Something you need to do right *now*, before this gets totally out of hand.
Go to C-26.

C-22

"Of course it is all lies," Dr. Nebs says. "This is the Night Office, after all. They don't want you to know the truth, because they fear it will destroy your mind."

"Even more than that time when I had to face that Mind Ripper from Outer Carpagenia?"

"Even more so than that time, yes."

"That thing almost convinced me that the Night Office was secretly trying to enslave humanity."

Dr. Nebs takes too long to nod in agreement.

"Are they?" you ask.

"Are who?"

"The Night Office."

"What about them?"

"Are they actually enslaving the human race?"

Dr. Nebs shrugs. "I only know what you know."

"And what I suspect."

"Well, I wasn't going to mention that, because it would be unprofessional of me to have such an . . . unsubstantiated opinion."

"Is that part of what this assessment is all about? Are they checking to see if I'm becoming . . . a liability?"

"Have you been co-opted by a shoggoth?"

"No."

"Then you aren't a liability."

"What if I don't believe the bullshit they tell me?"

"Don't let it get in the way of doing your job, is the best advice I can give you in that regard."

"That's helpful."

He offers you a pleasant smile. "Thank you. I'm trying to be helpful."

BEYOND THE WALLS OF SANITY

"I mean, I made you up, so I would expect you to be helpful—"
He starts to say something and then stops.

"What?" you ask.

"Actually, your psychological profile suggests that you would be more inclined to create a therapeutic personality that was antagonistic. In fact, the Night Office suggests that course of action."

"Do they?"

"They do."

"So if I was doing this right, I'd be doing what they want."

"If you want to look at it that way, yes."

"By making you all helpful and shit, I'm actually being a rebel."

"While that may be satisfying, that might not be the best option."

"What is the best option?" you ask.

"Do you really want me to answer that?"

"Yes, I do," you say. "I need to trust someone."
Go to C-76.

"No," you say. "I think you are trying to confuse me."
Go to C-84.

C-23

"I'm surprised," Dr. Nebs says when you open your eyes. "I had expected you to take the knife."

"No," you say, careful to not show any emotion. "Why would I take the knife?"

He studies you. "There's something you're not telling me."

"Probably," you reply. You do wonder much you can hide fro yourself.

He gives you a knowing smile—a cold smile. "We'll come back to that," he says, making a note. "How about we talk about your feelings instead?"

"Sure. Let's do that."

"Do you have a pet?"

"No," you say.

He taps his pen against his journal. "Don't be rude," he says.

"What?"

"I know when you are lying?"

"Regardless, that's not a topic I want to talk about."

"Why not?" he asks.

"It's private." You focus on the picture you have at your desk. The one-eyed cat. The one everyone asks about. You always tell the same lie. "Of course you do," Dr. Nebs says. "You have to maintain the illlusion. You have to make it real by saying over and over."

"Some like that."

"What about her? Did you tell the same lies about her?"

"Who?"

"*Her.*" Dr. Nebs puts enough emphasis on the word that there is no mistake about who he is talking about. "Are the two of you still . . . ?"

"We're fine," you say.
Go to C-88.

"Nothing lasts in this business," you say. "Especially relation-ships."
Go to C-90.

C-24

"This is unexpected," Dr. Nebs says when you stride into his office. He's sitting in his leather chair, like he does when he has patients, but there's no one—

(flash of movement out of the corner of your eye; was that someone leaping out the window?)

—in session with him right now.

"I had to see you," you say. You go over to the couch and examine the windows. They are all closed and locked. For some reason, the glass is highly reflective, and you see the room more readily than you can see outside. You look at—

(was it a reflection you saw?)

—and then turn away. You don't like what you see. There is madness in those eyes.

"Why don't you sit down," Dr. Nebs says. His hands are folded over his notebook and fountain pen. He doesn't seem terribly concerned. It's almost as if he is accustomed to these sponta- neous interruptions. "Tell me what is bothering you," he says. "I'm listening."

"I'm losing my mind," you say.

He raises an eyebrow. "How can you tell?"

"What do you mean?"

"You are experiencing some reality that is quantifiably differ- ent than your normal reality," he says. "There is something strange about the world, but you can't quite articulate it. It makes you uneasy. Makes you question everything. Makes you wonder what you are missing."

"What am I missing, Doc?" you ask.

He lifts his shoulders. "It's not my place to say," he says. "I am merely a witness. I am not a participant."

"You can't—or won't—make changes," you say.

He shakes his head. "These sessions are about you. Not me. I record your observations. I do not judge. I do not offer interpretation."

"But that's not what you write in your notebook," you say.

His lips tighten to a firm line. "My notebook is not for you," he says.

"Maybe it should be," you say.

You remember the knife, and you take it out of your pocket. It's a metal case with a small stud at one end. When you touch the stud, the blade springs out.

If he is concerned about the knife, he doesn't show it. You imagine you aren't the first patient to threaten their therapist with violence. He regards you calmly, waiting for you to make the next move.

Stab him already! He's waiting for you to do it!
Go to C-27.

Sense the calm radiating from him. You don't want to hurt anyone. You just want to understand what is happening.
Go to C-29.

C-25

"Alison Cambrie. You remember her, don't you?"

That bitch teased you mercilessly in high school. She was part of the cheer squad. Dated that guy on the basketball team. What was his name—well, it doesn't matter. She sat behind you in that one history class. Western Civilization. Taught by Mr. Hurley. He was a spineless one, wasn't he? His hands were always sweaty, and he always lingered in your row when he was handing back papers. It wasn't you. No, you were always buttoned up, collar pressing against your neck.

It was Alison. Tight sweaters. Short skirts. *That* Alison.

She liked calling you names. She and her friends, all gathered around their lockers at the end of the hall. You had to go past them after History, and no matter how you tried to slink past, hiding behind gaggles of underclassmen, she would spot you. Her catcalls would chase you down the hall, your face burning with embarrassment.

She knew.

She had caught you looking at her during home games. You didn't care about basketball. You barely understood the rules. But you never missed a game, did you? You were always there, high in the bleachers where no one would notice you. Where you could watch the cheer squad. Where you could watch Alison, in her tight school sweater and her short skirt.

And then, that night after a game where the team had been trounced rather fiercely by your biggest competitor, you had seen Alison and whatshisname arguing. It was late; it had been raining. He was angry about something, and he hadn't brought the car around to the gymnasium door, forcing her to walk across the lot. Her hair was wet, clinging to her face and neck. Her eyes were bright.

He was shouting at her, and when he put his hand on her arm, she tried to pull herself free. He wasn't happy about that. He grabbed her harder. She struggled. He pulled her toward his car. You don't remember what happened next, or you didn't see what happened because you were getting out of your car.

You remember the sound of the rain on the hood of the car. You remember the distant shush of traffic on the main road. You remember the gleaming whiteness of his skin, in the sodium glow of the lonely parking lot light. You remember the sound of her crying.

And you remember your hands, tight around the cold handle of your switchblade. Ah, you shouldn't have brought the knife with you. You knew better. But some deep animalistic reason told you to bring it to the game.

Later, when the police got involved, the story slipped out of your control. He said you had attacked both of them. That you wanted to steal Alison's necklace—the one he had given her not three weeks earlier. That you wanted to humiliate him. That was why you had threatened him. Why you had taken the necklace.

The necklace was nothing more than a tiny silver chain with a little silver cross on the end of it. He said you wanted a trophy. Something of hers.

What did he know about totems and trophies. Dumb fuck.

But still, you said nothing, and Alison said nothing, and so it was his story that went on the record.

You missed the rest of the semester, and when you were allowed to come back to the school, she wasn't there any more. Different school. Different state. It didn't matter. She was gone.

He remained. Even more of an asshole after that. After he saw how much power he had over you.

A year later, he slapped another girl.

You took the little finger of his off-hand. You weren't cruel. He was a star player after all.

Now *that* was a trophy.

"Yeah," you say to Dr. Nebs. "I remember Alison Cambrie."

"Good," he says. He scribbles in his notebook. "I was worried you weren't yourself." He smiles at you. "Space jellies have a hard time retaining host memories."

"Of course," you say, feeling a little flustered.

"Now, let's talk about the rest of your team. How did you feel about them during the mission?"

"Do you mean: did I like them?"
Go to C-31.

"Are you asking me if they were space jellies?"
Go to C-43.

C-26

The tiny bell jangles as you push open the door of the bookstore. You pause on the threshold. Behind you, the street is already fading into a fog that is too perfect to be real. Your mind is letting the past slip away.

It's okay. You can't go back anyway.

You enter the bookstore, and the bell jangles again as the door swings shut. There's something about that sound that tickles the back of your head. Are you forgetting something?

(what did you do during that last mission?)

The bookstore is as you remember it: warm, cozy, and filled with books. Mr. Fish is curled up in his basket. He looks half-asleep, but you know he is watching you.

There's no sign of the proprietor, but you know he's in the stacks somewhere. He's not worried someone will come into the shop and try to steal a book or rob the cash register. For one thing, there's no cash in the drawer.

Mr. Fish is all the security the store needs, anyway.

You wander over to the display case near the counter and rub your thumb against Mr. Fish's side. He yawns, showing a pink tongue and lots of sharp teeth.

The bookstore owner shuffles out from the stacks of books. He looks like a nattily dressed antiquarian. His glasses hang on a gaudy chain of tacky jewelry, and his hair is spectacularly windswept, which is a bit of a trick given he never leaves the store. He is carrying a tray with a teapot and two china cups.

"Ah, hello," he says brightly. "You are just in time."

Of course you are. This is how it always is with bookstores.

He sets the tray down on the counter and deftly pours tea. He offers you a cup and picks up the other. He blows on the tea for a moment and then sips noisily.

You follow suit. It's Lambent Sunrise, of course. Nothing too stringent or bitter. Just warm comfort.

"What can I help you find today?" He asks.

You put your hands in your pockets as you try to figure out where to start. There's something in your right hand pocket. You take it out and put it on the counter.

It's a switchblade knife.

He sips at his tea again.

"I'm a little concerned that I am carrying this around," you admit. "I thought that was all well behind me."

The corner of his mouth twitches, but he doesn't say anything.

"I'm not sure I'm on the right path."

The twitch is deeper this time, and there's a hint of something in his gaze as he regards you. Disappointment? Sorrow? Resignation? It's hard to tell, and you're probably projecting anyway.

"Where did you get it?" he asks.

You show him your hand. Look. There. A smear of blood on your index finger.

"Ah," he says. "You've picked a side."

"It would appear I have," you say.

"The right one?"

"I don't know," you admit. "Not yet."

"Are you going to disappoint them?"

You put your tea cup down. "What if they disappoint me?"

He shakes his head. "They undoubtedly will," he says.

"That's not helping," you say.

Mr. Fish makes a noise in his chest.

The bookstore owner puts his hand down and quiets Mr Fish. The old man sags for a moment, as if the weight of his cardigan is suddenly too much to bear. But he catches himself and finds a smile that will fit on his face. "It would seem as some time has passed since I last saw you," he says. "Your hair is different."

"I'm growing it out," you say. You don't bother to mention why. The official explanation of what happened in Carrisbane was an unfortunate explosion at the fertilizer plant south of town. The local population had been evacuated, and Heavy Battery had burned everything down to bedrock.

"You're older too," he says.

"That happens," you say.

He leans against the bookcase filled with all the ephemera that has recently caught his eye. You don't let the spines of the books distract you. "I may be in trouble," you say.

He raises an eyebrow.

You look around the shop again. It really does look exactly the same as the last time you visited. A dreadful realization sinks in. "You said I was older."

"You are," he says.

"That means you know me. That you've seen me before."

"Of course. Don't you remember me?"

You shake your head.

He looks mournfully at you. "Well, I suppose that is the price paid in your life of work." He finds a smile and puts it on, much like he was adjusting his glasses. "My name is Dalton Perth," he says. "I knew your aunt. You've been coming to my store since you were—" He puts his hand out at his waist. "Since you were this high." He smiles. "Do you remember the first book I caught you reading here?"

You shake your head.

"It was that naughty Baudelaire."

You feel a flush running up your cheeks. Ah, you remember that book, as well as who you bought that book for. Reading aloud to one another. Watching their lips move around the words. Watching them shift as they turned the page, a finger raised for dramatic effect. "That was"—you struggle to remember—"twelve years ago? Fifteen?"

"Was it?" He looks sad again. "I haven't seen much of you since then."

"I've been away."

He brightens. "Well, now you are back. What can I help you with?"

This whole thing has gotten weird and recursive, but you feel like you've stumbled into something safe. Something special. A place where you can be honest with yourself.

"I need—I need someone to talk to," you say.

Go to C-30.

"I need some direction," you say. "I have gotten off course, and I think I'm caught in some sort of tempora-spatial memory loop."

Go to C-33.

C-27

You remember stabbing Dr. Nebs, don't you? Where?

(in his neck)

In his office. As he sat in his chair.

(that's where you stabbed him)

No, you don't remember stabbing him. You remember seeing that he had been stabbed. That he was dying. That he didn't want you to read his notebook.

(why is there blood on your hand?)

And now, the room is cold. The corpse is old, desiccated as if no one has been in this room for a very long time.

(but you just stabbed him less than a minute ago, didn't you?)

Didn't he tell you something about memory loops? About getting trapped in your own subconscious when you are trying to outwit yourself.

(who are you lying to?)

"It's not like that at all," you mutter, turning the phrase into a mantra. *It's not like that at all.*

You look at the piece of paper in your hand. The words have gone wrong again, and you can't read them. You didn't trust them, anyway. You crumble the paper up, and leave it on the corpse.

You turn toward the door, but something catches your attention out of the corner of your eye. You turn back, and there is a closet you hadn't see before.

You approach the closet and open it. Inside, you find several shelves, and on the shelves, there are boxes. Not too big. Not too small. You find a framed painting on the lower shelf. The canvas is covered with a thick layer of white pint.

The painting is familiar. Have you seen one like it before?

If wish to examine the boxes, **go to C-100.**

If you think the painting is a reflection of the endless recursion of your insanity, **go to C-32.**

C-28

"The necklace that Brian Gerlacher gave her."

"Oh, was that his name?"

Dr. Nebs frowns at you. "You know his name. Don't pretend."

"I don't think that was his name," you say. "Is there someone in HAND named 'Gerlacher'?"

Dr. Nebs's nostrils flair. "No," he says.

"Are you sure?"

"We were talking about Alison Cambrie's necklace."

"Were we?"

"You're being evasive."

"I'm not sure that is possible. You are part of my psyche. How can I hide from you?"

"That's the very question I am asking myself," he says.

"See? We are simpatico."

"Then why are we having this conversation if we are thinking the same things?"

"Hey, I didn't ask for this. ARM said I had to talk this assessment so that PINEAL can clear me for the field."

"It will go faster if you answer the questions truthfully."

"I am."

"Then why are you pretending you don't recall Alison Cambrie's necklace. Or Brian Gerlacher."

"Look, Brian—or whatever his name was—was an asshole, back in high school. I don't know, maybe he's still an asshole. I don't care enough to find out. We had a talk—"

"A talk?"

"Yeah, a talk. He decided to test me." You shrug. "He found out what happens when someone doesn't believe me."

Dr. Nebs is quiet for a minute. "Are you testing me?"

"Do you mean, am I testing myself?"

He lifts his shoulders slightly.

"I'm me," you say. "I know that. Apparently, the Night Office wants me to prove it to them."

"How do you think you could do that?"

"Maybe I could tell a funny story or something?"

"Is that all?"

You spread your hands. "Funny stories go a long way."

Go to C-109.

"There should be some way I could prove myself," you offer.

He quirks his lips. "There might be," he says. "The Dark Labyrinth."

Go to C-75.

C-29

"Do you want to hurt me?" Dr. Nebs asks. "Is that what the knife is for?"

"Maybe," you say. Hedging your bet.

"Are you wondering if I am real?"

"Maybe," you say. Still hedging your bet.

"How will killing me answer that question?"

"That's recursive," you point out. "If I am imagining all of this, then I can certainly imagine killing you." You pause and think about it for a second.

"Maybe I already have," you say.
Go to C-4.

"But I see your point," you continue, "if I am inventing this experience, then there is nothing I can do to break out of—what do I even call this?"

If you think this is all just a very bad dream, **go to C-34.**

If you think this is all a nightmare that has been injected into your brain by space aliens in an attempt to stop you from doing something terrible, **go to C-35.**

C-30

"Maybe you should see your therapist?" Dalton suggests.

"How do you think I got there?"

He raises his shoulders. "I have no idea how you got here," he says.

You run a hand through your hair. This is all very confusing. "I'm—I'm not sure how I got here either," you say. "I was on assignment, and things got . . . complicated. I might be—I might be imagining all of this."

"Why?"

"What do you mean?"

"Why are you imaging this?" Dalton toys with his cup. "Have you suffered some sort of injury? Are you trying to find your way out of a maze? Have you been co-opted by an extraterrestrial intelligence?"

"Yes. No. Maybe. All of the above?"

He nods. "So you're fighting back. That's good."

"I suppose it is," you say.

"You're looking for yourself," Dalton says. "Trying to anchor your psyche on the things that are unmistakably you."

"So I'm going to revisit a bunch of my past in an effort to reconstruct my identity?"

"That's one way to do it," he says. "But you may also be feeding your past to whomever has assaulted your mind. Giving them details that will allow them to burrow deeper into your psyche."

"You're not helping," you say.

He pokes at the switchblade. "This is dangerous," he says. "You can just as easily use it on yourself as on someone else."

"I know," you say. "That's why I'm looking for some guidance."

"Get rid of it," he says. He hesitates for a second. "You're afraid, aren't you?"

"Of course I am," you say.

"Why?"

"Because of what I've done—no, because of what I might do. No. That's not it. Well, it is. I think I've done something, but I'm not sure."

"Have you killed someone?"

"Probably." You laugh. "It's an occupational hazard."

"Is that why you're afraid?"

"I keep thinking about a whiteness," you say. "A great blank. I don't know if it is in my own head, or if it is something else. Somewhere else. I don't know what it is, and I don't even know if it is supposed to happen or has happened already. But it's the nexus point. It's where all paths converge."

"Are you running away from it or running toward it?" he asks.

"Away from it," you say.

Go to C-36.

"Toward it," you say.

Go to C-38.

C-31

"Did you engage well with your team?" Dr. Nebs is curious about your answer.

"Well, we didn't kill each other on the front lawn, if that is what you are asking," you say. You can he isn't satisfied with your answer, and so you give him a little more. "Yeah, we were fine. We got in, did the job, and, ah, most of us got out alive."

"Who didn't make it?"

"Who do you think?"

"I don't know the particulars," he says. "Why don't you tell me?"

"Why don't you look in my head and see? I mean, you're part of me, so it shouldn't be too hard."

"There isn't anything to see," he says. "You're hiding it from me."

"I'm not."

"Why are you hiding your mission from me? Did you do something you shouldn't have done."

"We always do things we shouldn't do. It's part of the job."

He rolls his eyes. "Not like that. This is something serious, isn't it?"

"Maybe I don't want to talk about it."

"It's why we we are here. You have to talk to someone. You can't keep it all bottled up. No one can live with that much guilt."

"I'm not feeling any guilt," you say.

"Not now. But later. You will later."

"Or not, Doc. I may not feel it later. I may never feel it."

He regards you for a moment. "Is it like that then?"

"It might be," you say.

"Pity," he says.

"It's how we survive. It's how we make it through the day. How we manage to come back tomorrow and do this all over again."

"It will break you, eventually."

You shrug. "But not today."

"But not today," he echoes. Dr. Nebs closes his notebook and gets up from his chair. He puts the book in one of the drawers of his desk, and then he walks over to the door and opens it. "We're done here," he says. "You can go."

"That's it?"

"That's it. You shared a human memory with me. You expressed no regrets about your actions. You seem ready to go back to work. That's all we needed to know."

"But you said that I would crack. That I shouldn't bottle up my feelings."

"You shouldn't," he says. "But you have to, as a field operative for the Night Office. As long as you can."

You get up from the couch and walk toward the door. You pause near him. "This seems . . ."

"Unfinished?"

"Yeah, unfinished."

He gives you a cold grin, a shark smile that you recognize. It's the same smile the Old Man used to give you when you asked stupid questions. "No one gets closure in the Night Office," your therapeutic personality says.

IT'S THE ONLY TRUTH THERE IS.

MAPS SCORE: 74

C-32

Do you remember the sensory deprivation tank exercises? You spent hours floating in the dark, listening to audio tapes that were recordings of schizophrenics trying to convince you that you were insane. Why? Because some team of crack psychologists thought this was a good idea. *Identity Deconstruction*, they called it. You were supposed to learn how to maintain your own sense of self while bombarded with dozens of differing interpretations of reality. Fun, right?

Every year, a couple of trainees lose their mind during this week. It's not hard to guess why.

But you remember this week, don't you?

(did it really happen?)

They tried to tell you you weren't you. That you were confused about your sexuality. About who you thought you were. About how your family didn't love you. How they abandoned you. How their love for you was so totally fucked up. How everything you thought was true was actually a lie perpetrated by a vast conspiracy meant to keep everyone stupid and chained to their devices, sucking at an endless stream of vile totalitarian bullshit that was what the world stage had become.

Do you remember all of this?

(nothing but puppies and unicorns)

A Closer is an axis. They are a point upon which the universe will spin. They must be grounded. They must know what is true. They must be able to dismiss what is not true. They must know which way is up. That black is black and that white is white. That grey is everything in between, and yes, dear heart, you can be forgiven for all of your transgressions, but only if you are pure in your intent.

(get out! get out of the labyrinth!)

BEYOND THE WALLS OF SANITY

Once you start spiraling, it is nearly impossible to stop. The farther you fall, the harder it is to turn. To change your course and go in a different direction.

But it can be done.

So, are you lost, or do you know what you are doing?

You're a little adrift. Maybe you should rewind this. Back to a moment before you made a terrible mistake.

Go to C-102.

You need to get out of the Labyrinth.

Go to C-107.

No, you know what you are doing.

Go to C-41.

C-33

"I'm not sure I'm qualified to help you," Dalton says.

"No one is," you say. "I'm off the map in so many ways."

"Looking for monsters?"

"They're looking for me," you say. "But yes, I'm very much in those regions." You try to stop the laugh that is coming up, and manage to choke off most of it. "I need a guide. Or a marker. Or something. Before . . ."

Dalton nods. "Of course. Of course." He purses his lips for a minute. "Battillard? Spechza? No, no. It should be Oresti. Yes, that's it. Oresti's journals." He looks up, focuses on the shelves and then points. "There," he says. "Down Fiction. Past the 'L's, and then turn left. Into Philosophy. There's a shelf of vinyl records back there. Go past it and then into Geography. There's a cabinet back there, where all the atlases are stored. Start there. Look for Pedro Oresti's journals."

"All of them?"

Dalton laughed. "No, you'll be back there for years. Just the South American volumes. He did some work with faith-healers and visionaries. Up in the mountains. Down south."

A chill runs up your spine. "How far south?"

Dalton shrugs. "As far south as you can go," he says.

You figure that's far enough. "Okay," you say. "Down the fiction aisle. Turn left at 'L.'"

"Lingrenaldi," Dalton says. "Right there, at Lingrenaldi."

You take another sip of tea before putting the cup on the counter. "I'll check it out," you say. You scratch Mr. Fish behind the ears, and he makes a rumbling noise in his chest. You figure that's as good a blessing as you're going to get.

You wander down the fiction aisle, marveling—as always—at the collection of titles Dalton has for sale in his shop. Near the middle of the alphabet, there's a gap between bookcases—on both sides of the aisle—and you see more shelves running perpendicular to where you are standing.

You check the top shelf on your left. The first book is Lingrenaldi's *The Afternoon of the Causal Lion*. You've never heard of it, but that doesn't mean anything. There are lots of books you've never heard of.

You slip through the gap on that side of the fiction aisle. You're now in the Philosophy section. All you have to do is find is find the atlases . . .

Go to C-37.

You look at the book in the corner of the shelves on the right side of the aisle. It's a faded yellow hardback. Whatever title was on the spine has long since rubbed away. There's a volume by George Perec next to it.

You reach for the unmarked volume.

Go to C-39.

C-34

This is not a bad dream. This is an exercise intended to test your psychological resilience. You're not doing all that well.

If you're okay with failing, then you can certainly exit the exercise now. No one will speak poorly of you, but your record will reflect that, when given the opportunity to save humanity from eldritch horrors, you opted out.

Good luck with the rest of your life. We hope the nightmares won't last too long.

WE ARE NOT RESPONSIBLE FOR ANY REOCCURRING NIGHT-MARES THAT MIGHT PLAGUE YOU FOR THE REST OF YOUR LIFE. THAT'S YOUR OWN GUILT BUBBLING UP FROM YOUR UNCON-SCIOUS, WHICH KNOWS BETTER.

MAPS SCORE: N/A

C-35

You're right. This is a space alien spawned nightmare. Good for you!

Now, what are you going to do about it?

If you want to start over, because you feel like you're going to get it right this time, **go to the beginning of Section C.**

If you're still not quite sure of the rules, well, telling you the rules isn't one of the rules.
Go to C-108.

If you'd prefer to opt out and have a ham sandwich instead, **go to C-56.**

C-36

Dalton sighs. You've disappointed him. You want to tell him you aren't crazy, but where you do start? Do you even understand the full scope of what is happening?

(Has it already happened? Might yet happen? It's all very confusing, isn't it?)

Dalton grabs a notebook from the shelf behind him. When he turns around, he's not Dalton anymore. He's Dr. Nebs, and . . .

. . . you're not in the bookstore anymore. You're back in the therapist's office.

Dr. Nebs makes a note in his journal. "Well, this concludes our session."

"What—why?"

He gestures around his office. "All of this is a manifestation of your desire to run away. To flee from who you are. From what you must do."

"No, it's not," you protest. "I don't even know what I'm supposed to do—to be doing."

"You don't want blood on your hands," Dr. Nebs says. "But there is, and you want to hide the truth from yourself."

"No, I just want to figure out a way to fix this," you argue.

"You can't fix it," Dr. Nebs says. "That's what you keep failing to understand. You've opened one too many gates, and this last one is going to kill us all."

"No, that's not true."

"It is." He folds his hands primly in his lap. "They are coming, and you've shown them the way."

"But . . . but I didn't do anything," you say.

"Stop lying to me," Dr. Nebs says. "Stop lying to yourself."

"That's not . . ." You hear how plaintive and desperate you sound.

Dr. Nebs shakes his head sadly. He reaches into his jacket and pulls out a small revolver. Before you can stop him, he puts it to his head and pulls the trigger. It makes a tiny noise and he jerks to the side, toppling off his chair.

You leap up from the couch and rush over, but there's nothing you can do. Blood is soaking into the carpet. His eyes are wide and staring. There's an expression of horror fixed on his face.

He blames you, doesn't he?

You take the pistol from his slack fingers. It's an antique. A two-shot revolver from another time and place.

There's still another cartridge in it.

IT'S BEST TO END THE SCENARIO HERE. IF HE'S RIGHT—AND HE IS BECAUSE HE IS JUST A MANIFESTATION OF YOUR OWN GUILT—THERE ARE THINGS COMING. THINGS THAT ARE GOING TO TEAR YOU APART. IT WILL ALL END IN A RATHER UNSAVORY WAY. BEST TO NOT BE AROUND FOR IT.

MAPS SCORE: 6

C-37

You pass the shelf with the vinyl records. They're an odd mix of crooners from the mid-century, field recordings from places you've never heard of, and strange experimental records that pair disparate sounds together, like whale songs and vending machine error messages. You're about to move on toward Geography when you catch sight of a record that seems strangely familiar.

Les Fleur du Mal, as recorded by Gleebaus Bargleflee and the Midnight Sojourners.

You pull the sleeve off the shelf. The record is gray with dust. It'll need a good cleaning before you can play.

Someone has taken a black marker to the back copy, redacting it like a CIA black ops mission report that is—grudgingly—being submitted to a congressional oversight committee. All that is left are a bunch of effusive adjectives and a lot of verbs that are different ways to say the same thing.

The author's name is not blacked out. *Baudelaire.*

You hesitate for a second, and then tuck the record. under your arm. This is a treasure. This is what you were looking for.
Go to C-40.

This is a distraction, you think. *A bit of nostalgia for a world you no longer live in.*

Put the record back on the shelf and continue on toward Geography.
Go to C-48.

C-38

Dalton offers you a wry grin. "You were never one to run," he says. "That's why you were always in trouble."

"It's why you put up with me," you say.

"I always had a soft spot for troublemakers like you," he says. He taps the 'no sale' key on the ancient register on the counter, and the antique makes a muffled clang and shoots its drawer open. Dalton fumbles in one of the coin slots. "Here," he says, holding out his hand.

He drops a spherical object on your outstretched palm. It a series of concentric rings that are held in place by a central rod. You can spin them in alternating directions. There are markings on the rings, but they seem random and arbitrary.

"What's this?" you ask.

"A good luck charm," Dalton says. "Or some kids' toy."

"I'm not sure how this is going to help," you say.

He inclines his head. "You never know with the—"

"The who?" You don't quite catch what he said.

"Off you go," he says, waving a hand toward the stacks that extend into the depths of the bookstore. "Good luck."

You can pass on either side of his desk, which splits the bookstore into two sections: fiction and non-fiction.

Fiction, you think, chasing the lefthand side.
Go to F-2.

Non-fiction, you decide. *The righthand path.*
Go to F-4.

C-39

The book is covered in a material that isn't leather, but it isn't that fake leather made from old tires. There's a hint of a stain on the front cover, and you think about rubbing it off, but catch yourself at the last moment. There's no title on the cover, which means if you want to see what it is, you are going to have to open the book.

Seems like a trap of some kind, doesn't it? However, since you are deep in your own subconsciousness right now, looking for some clue as to why your brain has been compromised, this might be a clue. A hint? A lifeline?

You're flailing, aren't you? You hope this book is some kind of magical inner eye secret pathway or some other psychobabel nonsense. Go on, then. Open the book already!

The endpages are pretty and hypnotic. You have enough presence of mind to turn the first page before the mesmerizing fluidity of the abyss can suck you in.

The second page is blank. As is the third.

Is the whole book blank? Is this some sort of cosmic joke your subconscious is playing on you?

You start flipping pages, looking for something other than

(white rabbits in white snowstorms)

a blank page. As you flip through the book, something stirs in the gutter between the pages. It starts as a small flower caught in the binding, and as the pages turn faster and faster, it begins to glow. It sheds petals as it shuffles across the page. It sends out runners, which send out other runners. These tiny runners develop thorns, and they curl and curl and curl into a tangled mess at the bottom of the page.

You should stop flipping the pages, but the vines have grown so thick they are crawling onto the next page. They're wrapping around your fingers. The thorns are lacerating your flesh. You try to put the book back on the shelf, but you can't let go. The vines tighten around your hands.

The pages chatter. They are moving in a blur. Something is growing in the center of the book. Something with teeth.

You want to look away, but the vines have reached your shoulders. They circle your neck and start pulling. Bending you toward the open book, toward whatever is there, deep within these pages . . .

NOT ALL BOOKS ARE BOOKS. SOME ARE DISGUISES FOR MONSTROUS THINGS. NOW YOU KNOW, BUT IT'S TOO LATE FOR THIS VERSION OF YOU.

YOU CAN START AGAIN IF YOU LIKE, BUT TRY NOT TO WANDER TOO FAR OFF THE PATH.

MAPS SCORE: N/A

C-40

Dalton is surprised to see you. "Did you find what you were looking for?" he asks.

You nod, clutching your treasure to your chest.

He eyes what you have in your hands, and he seems like he's about to say something, but decides to hold his tongue. "I hope—" he starts.

"This time it will be different," you say.

"Very good," he says. He reaches under the counter and produces a black cloth bag. "Here," he says. "Don't go waving that around. People will wonder where you got it."

You take the bag and slip your treasure inside. "Thanks," you say.

Mr. Fish regards you with half-slitted eyes. It's the closest you'll get to approval from him. You'll take it.

Leave the store. All that remains is finding the way out . . .
Go to Section G.

C-41

So you think you know what you are doing? Well, where did all that blood come from, then? And why is your psychologist dead?

Oh, you made him up, so it doesn't count? Right. Right. That's what they all say. There's video footage that says otherwise. Would you like to watch it?

Yes.
Go to C-44.

No.
Go to C-45.

C-42

You can tell you're getting close to Geography when the biographies give way to books on sailing and trainspotting. You reach the end of row and step into an alcove. The back wall is surprisingly empty of bookcases, though there are a half-dozen stacks of books that are almost as tall as you are. You steer clear of them. They look like they're waiting to pounce.

On the right is a tall walnut cabinet with a heavy set of doors on the lower portion of the case. The upper portion of the cabinet is glassed in, allowing you to see the heavy atlases within.

There's a narrow door on your left. You missed it at first, but yes, it's actually there. It's short, and you are reminded of Alice's adventures in Lewis Carroll's imagination.

You're here for the atlases. Oresti's journals, remember?
Go to C-46.

That walnut case is solid. Those books aren't going anywhere. You have a minute to check out the tiny door.
Go to C-48.

BEYOND THE WALLS OF SANITY

C-43

"Well, if they were space jellies, then killing them was the right thing to do," you say.

"And if they weren't?"

You shrug. "The Night Office doesn't care about mistakes like that, as long as you finish the job," you say. "Saving the world trumps a lot of shit."

"Do you worry that attitude might put you at odds with . . . other members of the organization?"

"Not really," you say.

Dr. Nebs gives you a smile that says he knows exactly why. *Do you still have that finger?* his gaze asks.

I fed it to my cat, you eyeball him back.

You don't have a cat, he reminds you.

You smile, secretly pleased that you can hide things from yourself. *Good job, self,* you think.

"What if the Night Office cared?" he asks.

"Cared about what?"

"About whether or not you were sure people were space jellies before you killed them?"

"Well, what are they going to do? Send an auditor out in the field with every team? The rules are different once you start tuning the Way or opening portals to non-Euclidean spaces. We have to adapt. We have to make decisions—hard decisions."

"Like saving the world."

"Exactly."

"Why?"

"Why what?"

"Why is it important to save the world?"

"It's—" His question confuses you, and your confusion makes you angry. "It's my job," you say tersely.

"And if it wasn't?"
You don't understand his question.
"It *is* my job."
"Yes, but if it wasn't your job, would you save the world?"

"I, uh, maybe?" That doesn't feel like the right answer.
Go to C-92.

"No," you say. The truth is oddly freeing.
 Go to C-93.

C-44

A technician wheels in a video monitor. He puts it in front of you and switches it on. You feel like you should know him. Wasn't he the guy who briefed you . . . ?

Wait. How did you get in this room? Why are you shackled to this chair? This wasn't how it was. You were—no, wait . . . where were you?

As you struggle to remember, the video monitor switches on. It shows an office. It looks like a therapist's office. There's a desk, a comfortable chair, and a chaise lounge. There appears to be a broad bank of windows next to the lounge. A man sits in the comfortable chair. He is making notes in a notebook. There is no one else in the room.

He finishes with one page and starts writing on another.

You struggle. You are tied to a metal frame. Your ankles and wrists are bound with thick leather straps. There are more straps across your hips and chest. They are tight. You don't have a lot of wiggle room.

The man on the screen continues to write. He finishes another page. As he starts to turn the page, the image hiccups. He keeps writing.

When the image hiccups a third time, you realize you are watching a loop. It's not a live feed.

You look away from the video screen, and become aware of your surroundings. There is no . . . no room, really. It's just white nothingness. The cords from the monitor and stand trail off and vanish. You can't tell where the source of illumination is. It's just you, the frame you are tied to, and the monitor, which is running a never-ending loop.

Just as you're about to lose your mind, there is a change in the video. The man isn't alone. Someone else is in the room.

They are coming up behind the person in the chair. They have a knife. You struggle against the straps. You shout, even though you know they can't hear you.

The knife comes closer.

The man turns the page. The video hiccups, and it starts over. There is no one behind him.

You keep watching. You know the person with the knife will be back. You know you didn't imagine it.

THAT'S RIGHT. KEEP WATCHING. DON'T LOOK AWAY. DON'T EVER LOOK AWAY.

MAPS SCORE: 18

C-45

Dr. Nebs steeples his fingers and looks at you over the rim of his glasses. "The Dark Labyrinth," he says again. He waits for you to give him some sign that you know what he is talking about.

You sit there for a few minutes, trying to decide whether this is a test. Aren't you sitting comfortably in a chair at home? A glass of wine close at hand, the rain beating gently on the window. You've got your favorite slippers on. There's a fire in the—

"The Dark Labyrinth is the endless spiral your mind falls into as it suffocates from a lack of oxygen." Dr. Nebs's voice intrudes on your pleasant dream. "It is the path that leads to Endlessness," he says. "It is the last frustrating experience your brain will record before it shuts down. It is—"

"I get it," you say. "It's a bad place."

"It is *the* bad place," he corrects you. "Why are you down there?"

"I'm not," you argue.

"But you are here with me, and so . . ."

"What does that mean?"

He shrugs and makes a notation in his book. He frowns, crosses something out, and writes again.

"What are you writing down?" you ask.

"I'm making a list," he says.

"What sort of list?"

"Eggs. Butter. Salt. Goat blood. Strapping tape. I need to stop at the store on the way home."

"You can get all of that at the store?"

Your chest aches. It's hard to breathe all of a sudden. The room seems dimmer than it was a moment ago.

He doesn't answer. His pen keeps scratching across the page. *Scritsch scritsch . . .*

Your hands are heavy. It is becoming more and more difficult to move them. A heavy weight is resting on your chest.

"Butter . . ." you start.

Dr. Nebs looks up. One of his eyes is missing. There is nothing but a dark hole in his head. A hole you want to crawl into, even though you won't fit.

You still want to try.

"Eggs . . ." you say.

The hole gets bigger. Most of his cheek disappears. For a moment, you can see the roots of his teeth, but they vanish too as the hole devours the side of his face.

"Salt . . ."

When he nods, his head falls off. It wobbles across the floor, fetching up against the leg of the couch where you are reclining. You want to reach down and grab it, but your hands aren't responding to your demands. With a lot of effort, you tilt your head down and look.

You have no hands. That's the whole problem. Your arms end just past your elbows. You don't know where your hands have gone. Whatever cut through your arm did so cleanly; you didn't feel a thing.

There's a lot of blood all over the chaise lounge. You feel like you should do something about it, but what can you do? You don't have any hands.

You tilt your head back and look at Dr. Nebs.

He doesn't have a head. What a pair you two make.

YOU'RE GOING TO BLEED TO DEATH, YOU KNOW. THIS IS AN AWFUL WAY TO DIE IN A DREAM.

MAPS SCORE: 32

C-46

You inspect the walnut cabinet. It's easily as wide as your outstretched arms and a head taller. The lower section has two doors on it, and there is a light chain running through the handles. The chain is bound by an old keyed padlock, like something you'd see on a conquistador's chest.

The upper portion of the cabinet is also accessible by two broad doors, but they (and the rest of the upper cases) is glass, which, at the very least, lets you see what's in the cabinet. The upper section is locked with chain and padlock too.

Would have been nice to know about the padlocks, you think as you rattle the old locks. Neither accidentally falls open when you tug on them.

You look around for something heavy. Fortunately, there's no shortage of thick books on the nearby shelves. You grab one that has a unflattering picture of a train engine on the cover. It's as thick as your head and it's almost too much for one hand.

Use both hands and bang that book against the lock on the lower cabinet.
Go to C-47.

Use the book to attack the lock on the upper cabinet.
Go to C-49.

C-47

It's a little bit like swinging a sledgehammer. Once you start the motion, it's hard to stop. The book slams against the lower padlock and bounces off. You nearly drop the book on your foot. When you examine the lock, you notice the hasp is coming loose of the wooden housing. The lock itself looks utterly undamaged by your efforts, but if you smack it again, you might be able to knock the whole assembly off.

Hang on. Drop that book and you're going to end up with broken bones.

I'll be careful, you think.

Go to C-51.

Maybe you should reconsider this whole plan, and try something else.

Go to C-52.

C-48

It's a pocket door, and you jiggle the latch to open the door.

You wish you had a flashlight. You used to have one on your keychain, but you're not carrying your keys right now because you walked to your therapist's office, didn't you?

(Or is it because you're actually in a hospital bed somewhere, and you're missing more than your keys? Or is it because you're somewhere else entirely, and someone ese is in charge— someone who doesn't need keys to open doors.)

The room reminds you of a root cellar or a warren dug by some kind of nocturnal animal. The floor is packed earth, and there are roots sticking out of the walls. The room—well, let's call it what it is: a cave. The cave narrows at the back, and you think something might be huddled in the corner, but the shadows are deep enough that you can't be sure.

Forget it. You know a trap when you see it.
Go to C-46.

Aren't you curious? This is your deep subconscious, after all. What could possibly harm you down here? Isn't it possible that what you hope will save you from the mental break you're having is in the back of this cave?

Sure, it's possible, but . . .
Go to C-54.

C-49

Hang on. There's a lot of old glass on the upper portion of the cabinet. Are you sure you want to be smacking it with a heavy book? What if that glass breaks?

It's not going to break.
Go to C-53.

Oh, right. That could a bad idea. Maybe you should find a smaller book.
Go to C-52.

C-50

You know the statistics, and therefore, Dr. Nebs knows the statistics. Of the three people on a standard Asset Resource Management field operations team, Openers have the worst attrition rate. Followed by Guides. Closers are close to thirty percent. With the way the office rotation works, you don't get the same time very often. Working relationships are hard. Personal relationships are even harder.

"What about friends outside of work?" Dr. Nebs asks.

You laugh at that. After a moment, he joins you.

"I'm sorry," he says. "That was a silly question."

"The Night Office doesn't hire anyone that is well-adjusted or who can make friends easier. They want loners and outcasts, because no one will miss those sorts of people when they get their souls sucked out their nostrils or their brains popped."

Dr. Nebs doesn't disagree with you.

"Look, I trusted my team. You have to when you are out there. If you don't, it's likely that all of you will die."

"Isn't trust hard when one of them could be under the control of a space jelly?"

"Sure. That's why you have to be vigilant. That's why the Night Office wants me to take this assessment. You have to trust the people who work for you. If you can't, well, you're good and fucked. We're all fucked."

Dr. Nebs nods thoughtfully. "Do you trust me?" he asks.

"You're a product of my imagination, so I'm not sure if that question is even relevant."

He leans forward. "Do you want to know a secret?" he asks.

You look around, trying to figure out if this is some sort of gag.

"You're up for promotion," he whispers.

"What?"

BEYOND THE WALLS OF SANITY

"You are." He nods eagerly. "I can sense it."

"You're a figment of my dreaming mind. You don't have access to my senses."

"I'm more than I appear," he says.

"Somehow I doubt that," you say.

Dr. Nebuchenezzar looks around conspiratorially. "Listen," he says. "You have to trust someone, right? Why can't it be me?"
Go to C-74.

Dr. Nebs sits back in his chair and crosses his arms. "You don't believe me," he says, sulkily.
Go to C-95.

C-51

You swing the heavy book, and it hits the lock with a satisfying *thunk*. However, gravity has its grip on the book, and your swing continues right into your shin, which makes a very audible cracking noise.

Well done. At least you missed your foot.

You lean against the wall. Your leg hurts a lot, and when you glance down—ooh, that's not good. Your foot is floppy in a way that feet aren't supposed to be floppy. You're going to require medical attention.

A SHATTERED SHIN IS GOING TO SLOW YOU DOWN. YOU CAN'T OUTRUN SHOGGOTHS WHEN YOU'RE ON CRUTCHES.

MAPS SCORE: 42

C-52

You look at the stacks along the wall. Maritime shipping logs, a bunch of exotic flora catalogs from micro-nations you've never heard of, and repair manuals for old steam engines.

The last stack has a number of books about homesteading: making your own tools; growing your own food; killing in all the ritual ways. That sort of thing.

Nestled in this stack is a copy of *Metaphysical Lockpicking* by Durien Kennollipiae. You do that party game trick where you extricate an object from the middle of a tall stack without knocking everything over. You always were good at being patient and having a steady hand.

The book was published in 1928 by the E Ashmule Historical Invariance Society. Based in Boston. The book's lighter than you expected it to be, and when you open it, you discover why.

It's a fake book. Well, it used to be a real book, but someone glued the pages together and then hollowed out the middle. You've got a book like this at home, in fact, but yours was fabricated as a shell. This one is homemade. You're a little disappointed because the title sounded intriguing, but when you see what has been hid in the book, your disappointment vanishes.

Nestled in the compartment is a keyring with two keys.

Given the title of this book, you're not terribly surprised that the atlas cabinet would be hidden here.

Feeling clever, you return to the cabinet.

Use one of the keys on the lower cabinet.
Go to C-55.

Use the other key on the upper cabinet.
Go to C-57.

C-53

You smack the lock with the book. Nothing happens. You smack it harder. Nothing happens. You line up and smack it really hard with the book. And, well, lots of glass shatters. You were half-expecting this, so you let go of the book as soon as you feel it crunch against the cabinet. This saves your hands from the shards of glass. Some of it bounces off the nearby shelves. Some of it—

—Oh dear. You've got glass in your belly and in your legs. Oh, that's a lot of blood. No, don't pull it—

Now you've done it. That looks like a major artery has been cut. You're going to bleed out in less than a minute. Do you think you can find your way back to the entrance in that much time?

NEWSFLASH: YOU'RE GOING TO MAKE IT AS FAR AS 'F,' WHERE YOU WILL DISCOVER A FIRST EDITION COPY OF PETER FREUCHEN'S BOOK OF THE SEVEN SEAS. YOU'LL GET BLOOD ON THE DUST JACKET AND YOUR LAST THOUGHT WILL BE TO WORRY ABOUT HOW TOUGH IT'LL BE TO GET THAT STAIN OUT.

IT'S IMPORTANT TO REMEMBER THAT THE PHYSICAL WORLD CAN BE AS CRUEL AND NASTY AS FANGED MONSTROSITIES FROM DYING STAR SYSTEMS.

MAPS SCORE: 25

C-54

If you turn sideways, you can fit your shoulders through the door. Leading with one arm, you squeeze partway into the cave, reaching for the back. Your fingers brush something soft.

Almost there!

You strain a little more, pushing with your feet. Your hand moves a few centimeters farther into the hole. You can get a better grip on whatever this thing is and—

And it sits up and growls at you.

You panic and try to pull your hand back, but the creature is fast. It bites your fingers, and—*sweet mother of gherkin pickles!*—that hurts. You scrabble with your feet, trying to extricate yourself from the hole, but—

The pocket door has slid out of the wall. It's nestled against your belly. You can't back out, because the gap is much smaller now.

Your feet drum on the floor of the alcove. You try to snatch your hand away from the biting critter, but there's not that much room in the cave. It bites. It gnaws. Oh, it has a taste of you now. That's not good.

It—

WELL, YOU CAN IMAGINE WHAT IT BITES NEXT AND WE DON'T NEED TO DWELL ON THAT, DO WE? HOPEFULLY, YOU'LL PASS OUT BEFORE IT EATS YOUR EYEBALLS.

MAPS SCORE: 32

C-55

You unlock the lower cabinet. It's dark and musty in there, and for a moment, you hesitate, wondering if you are going to find feral mice or bibliophilic shrews nesting in the old books. Reaching cautiously, you hook the edge of one of the large folios that are resting in the lower cabinet.

The book tumbles out. It's in sad shape. The binding breaks when the book hits the ground and the cover sloughs off. The pages are a mess. Most of them are either overgrown with some kind of fungus that really likes paper and the dark. The rest have been gnawed heavily by those very mice or shrews you were worrying about.

The second and third books aren't much better. The farther down the stack you go, the better shape the books are in. It's all atlases. There aren't any journals here.

At least you know where Oresti's journals *aren't*, don't you?

Go to C-57.

C-56

A ham sandwich is tasty, and we don't fault anyone who picks it over a rigorous psychological profiling. However, in an hour or so, that ham sandwich will be gone, and the universe will still not give a shit about you.

Twelve hours later, you're going to crap out that sandwich, and then it'll be like it never happened.

The universe will continue to ignore you.

Vaguely satisfying, isn't it?

BUT AT LEAST YOU HAVE LEARNED THAT YOU PREFER A SANDWICH TO SAVING THE UNIVERSE. THIS IS A SIGN OF A SOMEWHAT BALANCED MENTAL STATE.

MAPS SCORE: 50

C-57

The lock on the upper cabinet is stiff, but you manage to get the key to turn. You have to yank the lock a few times to get it to open, but it does. You flip up the hasp and open the glass doors of the upper cabinet.

The books in this section are in amazingly good shape, considering how far back in the bookstore you are. You examine them carefully, peering at the spines. Most of them are hand-bound, and the markings on the spines are faded to near illegibility.

Near the bottom of the stack on the right hand side, you spot a trio of books that all have the name "Oresti" on them. Huzzah! This is what you were looking for.

You slide them out of the stack and place them carefully on the floor. They are folios, hand-bound and hand-sewn. The paper is heavy parchment. They are the original journals that Pedro Oresti made of his journeys in South America.

Your fingers tingling, you open the first one.
Go to C-58.

You're not sure what you're looking for, and so you trust providence and start with the middle journal.
Go to C-60.

You figure the last journal is going to have the info you need.
Go to C-62.

C-58

The first journal details his explorations of the Amazon Basin from 1946 to 1948. He was following the route taken by Henry Bates, nearly a hundred years early, when the English naturalist was exploring the great river. Oresti's journal is filled with watercolor paintings of trees and birds, much like Bates's journal must have been.

An hour later, you admit that it is interesting reading, but the most danger that Oresti has faced so far is drinking water from the river and getting swarmed by bugs.

Try the second journal.
Go to C-60.

Try the third journal.
Go to C-62.

You've read enough.
Go to C-64.

C-59

"Of course," Dr. Nebs says smoothly. There is a flicker of emotion on his face, but it doesn't last. "Do you feel that you were successful in the Closing?"

"I came back, didn't I?"

"That's not what I asked."

You think about his question for a moment. "Yeah, I think it was successful."

"Even though the rest of your team didn't make it."

"Well, I—sure, that sucks. But we all know the risks. We all know that—eventually—we won't come back."

"You didn't try to save them?"

"Of course, I did."

"Did you try hard enough?"

You keep your temper in check. "I resent the implication of that question."

"Which implication?"

"That I didn't try to save them."

"Are you feeling guilty about your effort?"

"No. Damnit. I'm not feeling guilty."

"So you liked watching them die?"

"That's not it at all," you insist.

"What is it then?"

You take a deep breath. You take several, in fact. "You're asking me leading questions," you say.

"Isn't that my job?" he replies. "Don't you want me prying into that part of your brain where you don't want to look?"

"Yes, but—no. No, that's not how this is supposed to work."

"Oh, so you know how it all works now, do you?"

"No, I don't know how it works. I just know that you aren't supposed to be so fucking antagonistic."

Dr. Nebs spreads his hands. "I'm part of you. Maybe you should examine the source of this anger."

"I don't—I'm not angry."

He cocks his head. "You see angry. Do you need to calm down?"

"I'm fine," you insist.
Go to C-63.

"I don't like this line of questioning."
Go to C-71.

C-60

The second journal looks more promising. Oresti is traveling down the Pacific Ocean side of South America, and he's getting sidetracked by rumors of strange medicines and esoteric cults. In one section, he travels up into the Andes to locate a tribe of Indians who still practice the old rituals. There's a holy ritual he hopes to observe, one that involves human—

The next dozen pages are torn out.

You flip through the rest of the journal. He makes some references to what he witnessed during that night when the "Voerdamnikenari" made contact with the Ithqua Inoxtl tribe. "I have seen beyond the edges of this world," he writes, "And I do not know how any of us can pretend that we are alone in the Universe. There are beings out there who would do us harm if they could reach us."

This sounds promising. You decide to check out the third volume.

Go to C-62.

C-61

"The Night Office has been dealing with shoggoths for over a hundred years," Dr. Nebs says. "In that time, the official directive has always been to burn them as soon as you can."

"Which makes it tough to do any, you know, field research."

"You're not a researcher. You're a Closer."

"Sure, but don't you ever wonder if we could—perhaps—shift the mortality rate of field operatives?"

Dr. Nebs folds his hands over his notebook. "Of course. Recruitment of new . . . flesh . . . is not very cost-effective."

"Exactly. Look at the Postal Service. They do very well with employee retention, and institutional knowledge is a critical part of keeping their costs down. The Night Office could do with a little more 'retention.'"

"Do you have something in mind?"

"We should capture a shoggoth."

"And how do you propose to do that?"

"We'd have to set a trap."

Dr. Nebs scribbles something in his notebook. His motions are fractured. He's agitated by this idea, you think.

"I am not agitated," he snaps.

"Why don't you want us to cage a shoggoth?"

"It can't be done."

"It hasn't been tried," you counter.

"It has," he snarls. "Many times. And every time, we've lost people. They are mindless. They exist solely to possess and devour. They can't be reached. They can't be reasoned with."

"Someone does," you say. "Someone tells them where to go. Who to eat. How to be patient and wait for us to find them."

"You think there is an intelligence behind them? Is that what you want to communicate with?"

BEYOND THE WALLS OF SANITY

"Sure," you say. "I want to talk to the space aliens."
"Why?"

"Because I want to make a deal."
Go to C-85.

"Because this war can't go on," you say.
Go to C-87.

C-62

The beginning section of the third journal is missing. The first actual page recounts an conversation between Oresti and a man in Concepción. How they met is part of the lost section, but the final part of the meeting of the meeting is there. The man (who appears to be some kind of local scholar) is telling Oresti about a group that is planning a trip to Antarctica.

"Go to Stanley," the man tells Oresti. "On the Falklands. They're going to the crescent of deception." Oresti notes that he must find a way to get on their boat. "It's the only way to—"

The next section is scratched out, but there's one word you can sort of figure out. *Voerdamnikenari.*

What kind of word is that? Is it Hindi? German?

The next entry is dated "September 18th, 1951," and it starts: "Today, I met Thaddeus Starkweather, and I knew I had found the key."

This feels like the jackpot. You find a spot on the floor, and with the book laid across your lap, you start to read . . .

When you are finished, **go to C-64.**

C-63

You feel a bit of a monologue coming on. You sit up on the couch and put your feet flat on the floor. "Look, I understand why the Night Office wants us to come in and have a sit down after a field operation. It's hard. We're Closers. It's likely we're going to be the only survivors of a job. It can be traumatic to see co-workers get eaten alive by tentacled monstrosities. It can be—"

You falter here. Not because you're emotionally bereft about what happened during the last job, but because you're still not ready to talk about . . .

You swipe at your eyes, dashing aside this moment of weakness. "We have to save the world. That's our fucking job. We have to Close the portals. We have to shut them out. We have to show the Old Ones that this world is not for them. We have to be strong—stronger—than everyone else. All the time. Does that take a toll? Absolutely. Do we know this when we go into the field. Absolutely. Do we do the job anyway? Abso-fucking-lutely. We are humanity's only hope."

You pause for breath. Dr. Nebs isn't taking any notes. There a tiny smile on his lips.

"Go on," he says.

You wave a hand at him and sink back against the couch. "Bla bla bla and hoorah," you say. "I know what the job entails. I know what it costs. I signed in blood, for fuck's sake. I don't need to sit around and talk about my feelings for an hour. I just need to go home, shower this shit off me, and drink until I forget it all. Can I do that now?"

Dr. Nebs taps his journal with his pen. "Sure," he says. "If that's what you want."

You look at him for a minute and then say, quite plainly, "Okay. I'm going to do that."
Go to C-94.

You hesitate. "There's something you haven't told me," you say.
Go to C-96.

C-64

The way back seems shorter than the way in, which isn't surprising. It is easy to be distracted in a bookstore by the other books clamoring for your attention. When you've found what you are looking for, all their plaintive cries no longer tug at your heart.

Dalton isn't in the front of the shop when you get there. Mr. Fish regards you with one eye from his perch. He makes a noise in his throat that isn't quite a purr and isn't quite a warning.

There are two doors out of this place. One is the glassed front door of the bookstore. You've seen it a million times, surely, and outside you can see the empty street. A car drives by. The other door is a plain wooden one. There is something painted on it— some kind of symbol—but when you try to focus on it, your gaze slips sideways.

That plain door doesn't want you to see it.

Mr. Fish stretches, showing you a mouth filled with too many teeth. He gives you no hint as to which door you should take.

Always inscrutable, that Mr. Fish.

So many doors. You are drawn to the glass door, but there's a lot of traffic out there. Even though it looks like the way out, it might not be. It might spin you around and send you somewhere else entirely.

Go to Section F.

Try the wooden door.
Go to C-70.

C-65

This is the opt-out section of this assessment. If you have come to this section by choice, then you are actively acknowledging that you have suffered some sort of mental break due to the strain of your last mission.

By opting to not continue with this assessment, PINEAL will have no recourse but to downgrade your Mental Acuity & Psychological Stability score. You are no longer qualified to be a field operative for Asset Resource Management.

It's okay. You're part of 99.99% of humanity. That's a very large community, and community is important.

It's too bad, however, that community won't ever understand why they're all going to die. They're probably going to be indifferent, unaware, or both when it happens. And while you can argue that being indifferent or unaware might be the best way to face extinction, it won't do much to change the fact that you'll be dead.

Well, good luck with the rest of your existence!

MAPS SCORE: 18

C-66

Dr. Neb shifts in his chair. "Am I? What makes you think you are worthy of a better explanation? Or that you deserve one?"

You encompass the room with a wave of your hand. "All this," you say. "If it isn't real, then someone made it. If my own dreaming mind made it, then it meant something to me. If I'm in someone else's dream, then they're working pretty hard to keep me caged. Why would they bother with that?"

He doesn't have a good answer.

You stand up and pace about the office. "It's one of those . . . what are they called? Black iron prisons. Yes, that's it. A black iron prison. A mental jail that is as insubstantial as reality, and equally as subjective. As long as I believe it is real, it will be real, but when I stop believing it, well, that's when things get dicey, don't they?"

Dr. Neb clears his throat. "Perhaps it isn't in your best interest to test this theory," he says.

"Why not?" You ask.

"Some theories aren't meant to be tested," he replies.

You have a high degree of confidence that he's bluffing.
Go to C-67.

You laugh at his answer. You both know it is total bullshit.
Go to C-69.

C-67

"How do I test this theory?" you ask. "That I'm trapped in some sort of mental prison?"

Dr. Neb frowns. "It's a theory that can't be tested," he says. "If I can persuade you this reality isn't real, then how do you know that I haven't talked you into a psychotic break?"

"That—that would be a bad thing," you say.

He nods. "And if this 'reality' is the fabricated one, why would I tell you that it is false? Isn't that counter to what you think I'm trying to do to you? I should be convincing you that this one *is* real."

"If you were doing your job, then, yes, you should try to convince me."

"Convince you of what? That this is real, or that it is all a terrible nightmare?"

"Now you're trying to muddy the issue further."

"This is what the Dark Labyrinth is," Dr. Neb says. "This is why it is so hard to escape from it. You don't know what is real. You don't know if I am real. You don't know if this is all something you're imaging, or if it's even more artificial than that."

"What do you mean?"

He waves a hand. "It's not important," he says. "What are you going to do?"

"I'm going to find my way out of this," you say.
Go to C-68.

"I'm going to find my way back," you say. "I'm not going to get lost again."
Go to Section C.

C-68

This job will mess with your head, the Old Man told you once. *You'll imagine things that aren't real. You'll be convinced that things you remember actually happened. You'll ignore other things because your brain can't figure out if they are real or not. Take me, for instance. I'm not even a part of this story, but here I am, giving you guidance. How fucked up is that?*

You try to ignore the voice in your head. It's just a voice, right? Dr. Nebs will attribute it to the psychotic break happening in your psyche. (*And whatever you do, don't tell him it's me you are talking to*, the Old Man whispers.)

Dr. Nebs notices your confusion and he watches you closely. You consider

(should I stab him now?)

telling him what is going on in your head, but that doesn't seem like a good idea.

Though, doesn't he know already? He's a figment of your imagination. A construct you were taught to fabricate so you had something to cling to when everything starts falling apart.

"I have to fix this," you say out loud. "I have to find the way out."

Yeah, good luck with that, the Old Man says.

Or maybe Dr. Nebs says it. It's getting hard to tell the difference between the therapeutic construct you were supposed to imagine and the one that has somehow infiltrated your psyche.

"Tell me how to find the Dark Labyrinth," you say. "I have to face this—whatever this . . . this trauma is."

"It's not really a labyrinth," Dr. Nebs says.

"Whatever," you say. "How do I find it?"

"It's already found you," he says.

This is where the bullshit starts, the Old Man whispers.

"Are you the Dark Labyrinth?"

Dr. Nebs smiles enigmatically. In your head, the Old Man doesn't say anything. Both are the answer you're looking for.

"I'm leaving now," you say. "You're just going to twist me up more if I stay."

Dr. Nebs makes a note in his journal.

You stand up and walk toward the door. You expect something to happen. Something that would prevent you from leaving the room, but you reach the door without any incident. You look back at your invented psychologist. He is writing in his journal.

"I thought so," you say. You reach for the doorknob and open the door.

Go to Section F.

C-69

This is the way it always ends up, doesn't it? You: pretending all of this is bullshit. Your therapist: nodding like he totally understands your frustration, but—*oh dear, I'm so terribly sorry*—there are rules he has to follow. Which leads to both of you not talking about the important things and skipping over the very matters you *should* be talking about.

On and on. It is always the same. It never changes. You save the world. You do the work. They think you've lost your mind. They put you through this visualization assessment. You place nice with your imaginary friends.

You know better, don't you?

You are sitting on the couch. You've been flapping your lips for ten minutes now, talking about your feelings. Dr. Nebs had heard it all before. Look at him. He's nodding and writing in his notebook. His eyes are half-closed. Overhead, the ceiling fan turns. You stare at it. Is it going counter-clockwise? Is that the direction it always turns? What was it that witches used to do when they were setting a spell, warding against evil. Ah, yes, widdershins. Counter-clockwise. Against the the direction of the sun. Toward the moon. Toward darkness.

Doctor Nebs's head falls forward, and a soft snore buzzes out of his slack mouth.

Ah, this is the moment, isn't it? When you can make a change.

You get up from the couch and walk carefully across the carpet. His notebook is loose in his hands, and you tug it free without any trouble. His hand twitches for a moment, as if part of him knows what you are doing—what you are *about* to do—but it's not enough to drive him back to the surface.

You page through the notebook. It's not just your sessions. There are session notes from other clients. You feel a twinge of guilt as you look over the psychiatrist's comments about your colleagues. Ah, here's a confirmation of what you've suspected about Wilson. He *is* a kleptomaniac. He always got shifty-eyed when you couldn't find a pen at your desk. And look, notes about Harominy. Yes, good old Harominy, who is terrified of old bathtubs and what might be lurking in them.

My god, these people are a mess.

Where are Dr. Nebs's notes about you. Yes, here we go. Your first session, eight months ago, shortly after that incident in the employee lounge. He asked you about a recent assignment. What did you say about it? You can't quite make out his handwriting. *Zelphe*—? Followed by the words *trauma, phantasms, grief*, and *cat*.

Cat is underlined four times. And there are two question marks after the word.

The following pages are filled with worm-like doodles, crawling through holes in the page. They're vaguely unsettling.

You flip past a page written in different colored ink. The handwriting is different too. It's all block capitals. And what you read makes no sense—no sense at all.

IF THEY FIND THE OBELISK, THEY WILL KILL US ALL.

A chill runs up your spine. It's a Guide's note. Someone was in the Way, and they looked into the future. Or maybe it was the past. It doesn't matter. They looked where they shouldn't have, and now you've seen it too. The path is locked. The Way is fixed.

Dr. Nebs makes a funny noise, startling you. You glance at him, and you are even more startled by what you see.

His eyes are open. There is blood all over his shirt and jacket. A switchblade is jutting from his neck. He stares at you, and when he coughs again, more blood spatters from his lips.

It gets on your clothing. And on the notebook too. You try to wipe it off, but it smears all over the page. The letters—the block letters—they've changed. They say something different now.

LEAVE NO WITNESSES.

That's not what it said before.
Go to C-74.

Is this a note from a Guide? Or is something in your subconscious? Something sensed, but not fully perceived.
Or, it could be a space jelly, telling you what to do.
Either way, you are in danger. You have to act quickly.
Go to C-72.

C-70

The wooden door isn't locked, but it is stuck. You yank on it a few times, but don't have any luck getting it to open.

Ironic, isn't it? Here you are—a Closer—and the way out requires you to *open* a door.

Well, perhaps this doesn't require special Night Office magics. Maybe brute force will work.

You rummage around behind the counter, looking for a crowbar or something similar. You find a copy of West-Rootherton's *Survey of Spectral Visitations in Colonial America, 1750-1785*, which is interesting, but it's too fragile to use as a hammer. Eventually, you find a heavy-handled butter knife, which will have to do.

Returning to the door, you shove the butter knife into the gap around the latching mechanism. You wiggle it back and forth as you lift and pull the door. It moves a little—progress!

You lean against the knife. It bends.

Mr. Fish makes a noise in his throat. He's staring at you, and there's a hint of malice in his steady gaze. You extricate the bent butter knife from the door frame. "Oh, now you're going to have an opinion about what I'm doing," you say.

Mr. Fish blinks slowly. You've seen him leap out of his comfy basket, pounce on a small rodent, swallow it, and return to his basket in the space of a few seconds. He only looks like he's indolent and lazy.

You indicate the wooden door. "I need to leave," you say. "And I'm going out this door. Okay?"

Mr. Fish shifts in his basket. He blinks slowly at you again.

It's not *No,* but it's also not *Yes.*

You half-turn, and when you slip the butter knife in the door again, Mr. Fish makes that noise in his chest.

"What am I supposed to do?" you demand. "The door is stuck. There's no key. I need to pry it open. This is just a dumb butter knife. I'll bend it back when I'm done, okay?"

He doesn't respond, and after staring at him for a minute, you decide to risk it. You shove the knife back in the crack, and ignoring Mr. Fish, you hammer the butt of the knife with your hand. Once. Twice.

Something cracks inside the latch. You pull the butter knife free and try the door. The handle turns. The door is going to open!

You bend the butter knife back to close to its original shape. Holding it carefully with two fingers, you approach the counter and put the knife down. For a moment, you panic when Mr. Fish shifts in his basket, but he doesn't get out. He's just getting comfortable.

You return to the wooden door. You're about to open it when Mr. Fish lets out a yowl. Your heart stops and you freeze.

Nothing happens, and you nervously look over your shoulder.

Oresti's journal—the book you were taking with you—is sitting on the counter. Right where you put it when you started rummaging around.

You were about to leave without it.

Embarrassed, you retrieve the journal.

Mr. Fish doesn't make a sound when you turn the knob of the wooden door. You pause before opening the door. "Thanks," you say to Mr. Fish.

Go to Section G.

C-71

"You are agitated," Dr. Nebs observes.

"Absolutely. I don't like your questions."

"Why not?"

"You think I'm not telling the truth."

"Well, I am a construct of your own mind, so I know when you are lying."

"Do you? This goes both ways. I know when you are lying too."

"Oh. You think I am the one hiding something?"

"Aren't you?"

Dr. Nebs smooths the crease of his trousers. "I don't think I am capable of such a thing," he says.

"You are capable of more than you are letting on," you say.
Go to C-66.

"I think you are part of an agenda," you say.
Go to C-79.

C-72

You tear the offending page out of the notebook. That's right. Don't let anyone know your intentions. Play this close. Get closer. That's what you do, right?

No, that's not right. This language is tricky. Get *closure*. Yes. That's what you meant. You are a closer. You get closure. You don't get closer. You are—

Wait. Why are you struggling with your words?

You smooth out the piece of paper you tore out of Dr. Neb's notebook, and the words are a collection of boxes and dots. It looks more like machine code or a language expressed in whistles, clicks, and hard knocks. You flip through the notebook. Every page is filled with the same script.

What is happening?

You struggle to remember how you got here, and it's all very murky. There was a special assignment, wasn't there? Somewhere cold. You remember going somewhere cold.

You're all alone in this room. The furniture is tidy and spartan. There is a painting on the wall, except the canvas is nothing but layers and swirls of white oil paint.

There's a mummified corpse sitting in a chair near a low couch. It's wearing a suit, and its skin is mottled and stretched tight across the bones. There is something stuck in its throat, and when you peer closer, you see it is a knife with a thick handle. A switchblade of some kind.

That knife is familiar, but you can't place it. Where did you get it? You struggle to remember. It's so hard.

There's something caught in the corpse's mouth too. The jaw is stiff. You pry it open and tease out a crumpled piece of paper. It is from the same notebook. You smooth out the piece of paper and discover writing on it, writing you can read.

IF THEY FIND THE OBELISK, THEY WILL SAVE US ALL.

That's not what it said before, you tell yourself.
Go to C-80.

Can we talk about how you only killed Dr. Neb a minute or so ago, and now he's mummified as if no one has come into this room in, like, eighty years? That's not normal.
Go to C-27.

C-73

Dr. Nebs puts his pen down and closes his book. "This is very troubling," he says. "I had hoped for better engagement."

"What are you talking about?"

"Denial," he says flatly. He goes over to his desk.

"I'm not in denial," you insist. "I'm just having some trouble adjusting to the shifting parameters of reality."

"That's what all my patients say," Dr. Nebs says. "Before . . ." He opens a drawer and frowns at what he doesn't find.

"Before what?" you ask.

"Ah." Dr. Nebs has opened another drawer. "Here it is."

He lifts something out of the drawer. It writhes and twists around his hand. Tentacles snake up his arm.

"What the fuck is that?" you say. You scramble onto the couch, getting your feet off the floor,

(it won't make any difference)

Dr. Nebs points the writhing thing at you. It pulses and vibrates, and somewhere you can hear something screaming.

"It's a Mind Killer," Dr. Nebs says flatly. His face has gone slack, and his eyes are dead. When he walks, he moves as if he doesn't quite remember how his legs work. "Didn't they tell you?"

"No . . . No, they didn't."

"Pity," he says. He's drooling, and it only gets worse when he smiles. "Hold still. This won't—"

The tentacles lash out from his fist.

WE ADMIT THIS ENDING MAY HAVE ARRIVED ABRUPTLY AND UNFAIRLY, BUT THE UNIVERSE CAN BE LIKE THAT.

Try again.
Go to Section C.

C-74

This is what the assessment is all about, isn't it? You've just finished a job for the Night Office, a job where you may have encountered a shogggoth. Shoggoths are always trying to infiltrate the Night Office. While they are the most mutable of the extra-terrestrial intelligences available to the Great Old Ones, they aren't the smartest. They can get into the human brain and rewire it fairly quickly, but they aren't very good at operating the human body. You can usually spot one pretty easily.

At least, that's been everyone's experience. What keeps the Night Office awake at night is the fear that shoggoths are going to get smarter. That you won't be able to tell when they've infiltrated someone.

Which is why these assessments are a critical part of the debriefing process following a successful field operation. It is important to know that what comes back from the field is just as human as what went out. Though, some will argue that these assessments are too hard for normal humans, but that matter is still under review by HAND and upper management.

Of course, none of that is relevant right now, because you're trapped in the middle of this byzantine construct you're own brain has created. Yes, it's very much a black iron prison, isn't it? You don't know who you can trust, do you? It's even worse than that, because all the characters you've met so far are of your own creation. You're fighting yourself, and the more you fight, the more your training kicks in. The more your instincts tell you to flee. You doubt yourself. You doubt your sanity. You doubt that reality is even real. Maybe it is all a dream. Or a psychosis. Or who the fucks knows really?

One thing is for sure: they aren't paying you enough.

Anyway, much like you do in the field, you need to push aside all these confusing thoughts. You need to focus on that kernel of identity that is *you*.

Good. Now put that kernel in a room. Give it some legs. Arms, too. Put a head on it. Give it some hair. Excellent.

Now, imagine two doors out of this room. They are marked "What I Know" and "What I Feel." They are the only ways out of this room, out of this mental prison. You have to pick one, but they both lead to the Dark Labyrinth.

You have to make a choice. The more you fight entering the Dark Labyrinth, the more your brain devours itself. The recursion loops come from these holes in your brain. It's almost like stepping into the Way, but in an entirely subjective manner.

Anyway, pick already. Things are going to get weirder.

What I *know*.
Go to Section F.

What I *feel*.
Go to C-26.

C-75

"The Dark Labyrinth is a mental construct that exists on a deeper level of consciousness than we are right now," Dr. Nebs says. "It was programmed into you via subliminal neuro-linguistic hacks during Orientation & Inoculation. It resembles an endless library—after Borges, of course. Shoggoths can't navigate it, because they don't have the proper attenuation of imagination. Humans can. It is the final aspect of this assessment."

"What am I supposed to do?"

"You're supposed to find your way out of it," he says.

"And if I don't?"

He lifts his shoulders. "Then you must be a space jelly."

"I don't think that is a proper equivalency," you point out.

"It won't matter. You won't be around to argue the case."

"And is that how I get out of this . . . this mess?"

"Well, this mess is of your own creation, so you should speak more kindly of it."

"Whatever. Is that the way out?"

"It is."

"And how do I get there?"

He lifts his pen and points the end of it at the couch you are sitting on. "You fall through that."

"What? The couch?"

"Yes, the couch."

"Like . . . I just fall?"

"Well, it looks like a sucking motion from over here, but to you, yes, it will feel like falling." He taps his pen against his teeth. The noise rattles you. The sight of his teeth rattle you.

"I think you're lying," you say.
Go to C-66.

Remain calm. Get comfortable. Try to relax. Don't think about the shape of your therapist's teeth.
Go to Section F.

C-76

"Having trust issues is almost a prerequisite for working at the Night Office," you say. "It attracts all sorts of outsiders, loners, and malcontents. We're all solitary losers with a mean streak of paranoia as our only true friend."

"And yet, the Night Office expects you to work together."

"Yeah, they do, don't they?"

"Do you think that is foolish of them?"

"There are easier way to get people to bond."

"Is there?" Dr. Nebs raises an eyebrow. "Why haven't you tried them?"

"I—I don't like people all that much."

"So you don't think companionship is important?"

"I didn't say that."

"Why don't you like other people? Does it have to do with your parents?"

"I thought you were supposed to be helpful?"

"No, you thought I was supposed to be helpful. I'm inclined to think otherwise."

"But you're a mental construct. You don't have thoughts of your own."

"Which brings me back around to my initial question: who should you trust? Your team? Yourself?"

"You know, this is one of those times when I see why I annoy people," you say.
Go to C-97.

"You're just trying to confuse me," you say.
Go to C-83.

C-77

"Yeah, there was a man on the team. He was our Opener."

"Did you like him?" Dr. Nebs asks.

"I don't like most of them."

"Who? Openers?"

You shrug.

"Was there a problem during this operation?"

"Other than space jellies, trans-dimensional entities, and sex demons from the Burning Lands, no. No problem."

"That's good." Dr. Nebs makes a note. "Are you dating?"

You laugh. "Define 'dating'?"

"Seeing someone regularly."

"This job doesn't allow for much 'regular,'" you remind him. "How about you? You seeing anyone?"

Dr. Nebs gives you a patronizing smile. "I'm a thought experiment," he says. "I don't date."

"Too bad. You're a bit too passive-aggressive for my taste, but otherwise, you seem 'normal.'"

"Unlike you."

"How so?"

"You are very passive-aggressive."

"Well, that's what talking to yourself will get you."

"Perhaps you should make some friends."

"Maybe," you say. "Once the world is saved."

Dr. Nebs makes another note. "So, Wednesday?"

"Sure. Wednesday is fine."

That's an office joke. *Hey, when is the world going to be saved? Oh, probably by Wednesday. Gotta make sure the weekend is clear.*

"So . . . no problems with the team?"

"No more than they with me."

"That's precisely what I was talking about," he says.

You give him a cold smile.

He sighs and closes his notebook. "I see how this is going to go. Perhaps we should get to it then."

"Get to what?"

"The other part of this assessment."

"What?"

"PINEAL believes that deeper immersion in your subconscious is necessary to generate a more accurate MAPS score."

"Well, that's fucking wonderful. How does that work?"

Go to C-75.

C-78

"Yeah, one. There was a woman on the team."
"And?"
"We've worked together before."
"How did it go this time?"

"It was fine," you say.
Go to C-88.

"It—the job got in the way," you say. "Like it does."
Go to C-90.

C-79

"An agenda? Me?" Dr. Nebs scoffs. "How could I possibly have an agenda?"

"This assessment is meant to test my mental stability," you say. "It is supposed to probe my shadow—my animus—and see if I am still whole, or if something has corrupted me. Because the Night Office does not suffer corruption, does it?"

Dr. Nebs has gone very still. "No," he says quietly. "They do not."

"What do they do with corruption?"

"They cut it out," he says.

"Is that what I am supposed to do if I find it?"

"Do you want to cut it out?" he asks.

"You're talking about self-harm" you say.

"It's not self-harm if you are saving the universe."

"It is, if there is no reason for me to harm myself."

"I'm not asking you harm yourself," Dr. Nebs says.

"You're *not* not asking me," you point out.

He pinches his lips together. His pen scritsches across the page. You notice that his left foot is wiggling.

"Are you nervous?" you ask.

"No," he says. He stops writing and looks up at you. "I dislike the sight of blood."

"Is there going to be blood?"

He sighs. "There always is."

You know you could change this scenario at any time. You have the power.

That's right. And if he wants blood, maybe that's what you want.

Go to C-81.

You are supposed to trust him, but isn't that the whole point of this assessment: to figure out whether or not you can trust yourself?

Go to C-83.

C-80

The problem with she said / she said arguments—especially ones you have with yourself—is that there's no right answer. There's merely the answer you choose and the other one, which is probably more "right" in some metaphysical sense, especially if the one you picked turns out to be, without a doubt, the wrong answer.

This path, by the way, was the wrong answer.

Why? Because you've spent so much time trying to unravel your own psychosis that you've forgotten a key fact of your psychic identity. You don't remember who you are.

Sure, go ahead and try. Start over—if you can. It won't matter. You think you'll do better this time around, but you're going to make the same mistakes, aren't you? You going to trust the wrong people. You're going to take the wrong turn when you come to a fork in the path, and the Way is going to get dark faster than you expect.

It always does, doesn't it?

Face it: you fucked up. You got lost in the recursions and now you don't know which of your shattered personalities to believe. Are you going to burn the world down?

No? Because that's not who you are.

That's an adorable conceit, by the way. Hold tight to that.

The first thing they teach you at the Night Office is that the human mind is a fragile identity construct that is constantly telling itself that electrical impulses constitute "life." And this identity—this "you"—can be co-opted by much smarter and much more malignant consciousnesses. You'll never know you've been turned. Even when they walk you into the open mouth of a Rhezzlanoria Nightmare.

Anyway, the point is that who you *were* is irrelevant.

Who you are—right now—is all the Night Office cares about. Is this person—this "you"—still human, or have you been turned into an ambulatory meat sack by a space jelly?

Now, look, you could fight to re-establish control. Shout your barbaric yawp and all that. *Let me try again!* you protest. Sure. We'll let you do that. All you have to do is go back to the beginning.

Ah, we see your confusion. *Which* beginning? That is the tricky part, isn't it?

You mean well. You want to be helpful. You want to do the right thing, but . . .

IT GETS COMPLICATED QUICKLY, DOESN'T IT? DO YOU REALLY KNOW WHO IS TELLING YOU WHAT TO DO? IT'S NOT US ANYMORE, WHICH CAN ONLY MEAN THAT YOU'RE UNDER THE THRALL OF SOMETHING ELSE.

AND THAT'S NOT GOOD.

MAPS SCORE: 24

C-81

You wander over to the large painting. It's a white canvas, covered with white oil paint. Up close, you can see cracks in the paint. You can see where the artist's brush left lines in the paint. There are ridges and valleys. Up close, it becomes a landscape filled with shadows.

Is this a metaphor for the human mind? Perhaps. It may be an illusion. This may all be an illusion. You may be sitting in a room somewhere—a room that doesn't look anything like Dr. Nebs's office—reading this assessment. Making choices. Looking for a path through your own tangled consciousness.

Why is this so hard? Are you hiding something from yourself?

Or is someone else trying to hide something from you.

You turn around. "Excuse me?"

"I asked if you thought someone was hiding something from you," Dr. Nebs says. "And if so, who?"

"What do you mean?"

"Who else is part of this assessment besides you and me?"

"There isn't anyone else."

Dr. Nebs turns in his chair and looks at the door to his outer office. "Are you sure?"

You look at the door. Is it locked?

"I didn't lock it," Dr. Nebs says. "Did you?"

Maybe you should check the door.
Go to C-82.

He's making you paranoid. No, wait. You're making yourself paranoid.
Go to C-84.

C-82

You go to the door of Dr. Nebs's office. It wasn't locked. Good thing you checked, right?

You pause before you throw the latch.

If you do this, are you locking yourself in? Are you shutting the cage door on that black iron prison?

You look back at Dr. Nebs. He seems unconcerned.

Locking the door is a trap. Another fucking trap. This assessment is full of them.

Go to C-84.

"I'm not locking myself in with you," you say. "In fact, I'm leaving."

You open the door and walk—

Go to C-26.

C-83

"You are making me doubt myself," you say.

"Am I?" Dr. Nebs looks wounded. "Why would I do that?"

"You are supposed to help me. I need to find a way out of this mental conundrum that I've—apparently—built for myself."

"You haven't even found the door yet," Dr. Nebs says.

"What door?"

"The door to the Dark Labyrinth."

"Why would I want to go there?"

"That's where all the fucked up little children of the Night Office go when they think they are broken," he says.

"I'm not broken," you insist.

He shrugs, as if doesn't matter what you think.

You look around his office. There is only one door: the door you came in. That can't be the door he's talking about . . . ?

"Not all doors look like doors," he says. His smile is patronizing.

You want to hurt him—distantly, you see yourself doing so—but you hold your anger in check.

There's something odd about the wall opposite your couch. You wander over to it, and when you get close, you realize that it isn't just a wall. It's actually a painting, made to look like a wall. It's only when you get up close that you can see the individual brush strokes. The blobs of oil paint.

"What is this?" you ask.

"It's nothing," Dr. Nebs says.

"It's everything," Dr. Nebs says.

You hear him twice, and there is a vast difference between the two voices.

"Not all doors look like doors," you whisper.

You reach out and touch the painting.

It's nothing. You feel like you could fall through it into another memory entirely.
Go to C-20.

It's everything. You feel like it could be a doorway.
Go to C-26.

C-84

"You're trying to make me doubt myself," you say to Dr. Nebs.

"I think you're doing a fine job without any assistance from me," he says.

You walk over to his desk. It's tidy and neat. There is a blotter, a phone, and a picture frame. You try to focus on the image in the frame, but it is blurry. No matter how hard you try.

You open the desk drawer. There is a tin of mints, some pens, a couple paper clips, and a stack of message pads. And a letter opener.

No, wait. That's not a letter opener.

It shivers under your touch, becoming something else.

You click the button on the handle of the switchblade and the blade pops out.

"What have you found?" Dr. Nebs asks. His back is to you.

"Something I buried a long time ago," you say.

"Are we digging up old trauma now?" Dr. Nebs asks. He still hasn't turned around. "My, we are spelunking in your psyche now, aren't we?"

Your grip is tight on the knife.

What are you going to do with it?

It's too late. You've already done something terrible.
Go to C-27.

This knife has a history. You can't escape it.
Go to C-86.

C-85

"What do you mean by wanting to make a deal? Do you want to negotiate some kind of truce?"

"God, no. That's a waste of everyone's time. Besides, I'm sure the concept of peaceful cooperation is completely alien to these . . . uh, aliens."

"So, who do you want to talk to?"

"Middle management."

"Excuse me?"

"I want to talk to whoever is running the space jelly program. It's not the big guys. It's someone in between. Someone who might have dreams, aspirations. I mean, running the jellies might be akin to—I don't know—managing gerbils over here. Something like that. No one wants to be the guy who runs a gerbil farm."

"Perhaps it is a satisfying job."

"Yeah, perhaps it is."

"You don't believe me."

"No, I don't. Middle management is always interested in moving up. They're aggressive about not being at the bottom of the middle. Perhaps we can work a deal."

"That's very . . . "

"It's out of the box thinking is what it is, Nebs. I thought the Night Office likes that sort of thing."

A CURIOUS PROPOSAL. YOU SHOULD BRING IT UP TO YOUR CASE MANAGER—WHO, BY THE WAY, IS MIDDLE MANAGEMENT.

MAPS SCORE: 74

C-86

Dr. Nebs turns around and looks at you. "Are you going to repeat your past mistakes?" he asks. His gaze drops to the knife in your hand. "Or are you going to make new mistakes?"

He grins, and when his lips peel back, you see how sharp his teeth are.

Deep, deep in your brain, something uncurls. It is some primitive part of your brain. It doesn't think. It only acts.

Fight?
Go to C-89.

Flight?
Go to C-26.

C-87

"Why can't this war go on?" Dr. Nebs asks.

"We can't win it. Not like this. The Night Office can't get enough operatives in the field. Not to mention the attrition rate. The Great Old Ones have been doing this for millennia. They can keep squeezing space jellies through holes in time and space forever. One out of three kills a Night Office operative. You do the math."

"So you think the Night Office needs to do something . . . more aggressive?"

"I do."

"Interesting." Dr. Nebs writes for awhile in his journal. "What did you have in mind?"

"Oh, you know what I have in mind, Doc."

Dr. Nebs frowns. "That's highly unorthodox."

"This is the Night Office," you remind him. "Everything we do is unorthodox."

THIS IS, INDEED, AN UNORTHODOX ENDING TO THIS ASSESS-MENT. YOU SHOULD CONTACT SOMEONE IN LABYRINTHIAN OBSERVATION & BYZANTINE ELUCIDATION IMMEDIATELY.

MAPS SCORE: 78

C-88

"You've been saying that often in this session," Dr. Nebs says.

"What? That I am fine? Well, I am."

"Are you sure?"

You give him a look, and he holds up his hands in defeat. "Okay, okay," he says. He closes his journal and stands up. "I think we're done here," he says.

"We are?"

He nods. "I can only ask you the same question so many times before I stop being useful, and I think we've reached that point in our conversation." He indicates that you should get off his couch. "It's time for you to go to the next stage of this assessment."

"There's more to this?"

He ignores your tone.

"You can either submit to the Dark Labyrinth for the final portion of this test, or you can leave now."

"But . . . ?"

"But what?"

"Isn't there a catch?"

"Would I lie to you?"

"Absolutely," you say. "I do it all the time."

He grants you that point, but he's not willing to give you any more of a hint.

"Fine," you say, and it isn't lost on you how he's turned that word against you.

Submit to the Dark Labyrinth.
Go to Section F.

Leave the session.
Go to Section G.

C-89

That's right. You're going to fight back.

The knife is the only friend you need.

Dr. Nebs leaps out of his chair. His skin is sloughing off. There's darkness underneath. Darkness and eyes.

Your grip is solid. You are on familiar ground now. You know what to do.

WELL, WE'RE A LITTLE DISAPPOINTED THAT YOU KILLED YOUR THERAPEUTIC PERSONALITY. IT SORT OF DEFEATS THE PURPOSE OF THIS ASSESSMENT. HOWEVER, THIS OUTCOME IS, UNFORTUNATELY, FAIRLY STANDARD FOR FIELD OPERATIVES WHO HAVE ENCOUNTERED TENTACLED AND FANGED MONSTROSITIES FROM OTHER DIMENSIONS.

HAZARDS OF THE WORKPLACE, WE SUPPOSE.

MAPS SCORE: 68.

C-90

"I'm sorry," Dr. Nebs says. "I know how much you cared about her."

"It's okay," you say. "We both knew what the likely outcome was." You struggle with your emotions. "We tried," is all you can manage.

"That's enough," he says quietly.

You shrug. It isn't. Not really. But what else can you hope for in this business? No one lives forever. It chews everyone up, sooner than later. There's almost no point in trying . . .

Dr. Nebs clucks his tongue and wags a finger at you. "Don't spoil it," he says.

You think about the other secrets you have. The ones he hasn't found. You've buried them deep. You bite your tongue and keep silent.

Dr. Nebs finishes writing his notes. *Scritsch scritsch* goes his pen, and then it falls silent.

"We're done," he says.

"We are?"

He stands up and goes over to his desk, where he pulls open one of the desk drawers. "There's just a little more paperwork to deal with," he says.

"No," you argue. "No more paperwork."
Go to C-113.

"This is what is going to kill me," you say. "All this fucking paperwork."
Go to C-115.

C-91

"How do I know whether or not I'm insane?" you ask your therapist, half-expecting him to give you another nonsensical answer.

"How many times have you asked me that question?" he asks you in return.

See? No surprise there.

"Often, I suspect," you say.

"Maybe you should try something else?" he says.

"Like what?"

"You could look out the window," he says. "You never look out the window."

Go to C-6.

"You haven't said anything about my new painting," he says. He indicates a large white painting on the wall behind you. You admit that you never noticed it before.

Go to C-81.

"Or maybe you should start over," he says. "Again."

Go to Section C.

C-92

"Fair enough," he says. He writes one more note before closing his notebook. "Are you afraid?" he asks.

"Afraid of what?"

"Afraid of what might be lurking in your brain?"

"There's nothing lurking in my brain."

"Are you sure?"

You start to answer and then stop. You settle for a shrug instead.

He nods as if this was expected. "I think you aren't quite ready yet."

"Ready for what?"

"You are hiding something. We should find out what that is, and why you think it is important to obscure it."

"I'm not hiding anything," you protest.

"Should we examine another memory from your past?"

"Oh, this'll be fun." You try not to roll your eyes.

Recall a memory from your early days at the Night Office.
Go to C-20.

Stall for time.
Go to C-81.

C-93

"Does that make you a psychopath?" Dr. Nebs asks.

"No, it makes me a realist," you say.

He grants you that one with a tiny nod. *Scritsch scritsch* goes his pen. You want to take it from him and . . .

"Do you want to stab me with my pen?" he asks.

"A little," you admit.

"Do you think that is a healthy feeling to have?"

"I think admitting that I am having this feeling is healthy."

"Yes, I agree with that." He pauses for a moment. "Are you?"

"Am I what?"

"Going to stab me with my pen?"

"Maybe later," you say. Mostly to be annoying.

"We should wrap up this session then," he says. "Are you ready for the next portion of this assessment?"

"There's more?"

"Of course. Talking with me was merely a means of getting you settled. Now you are ready for the next part, where you have to wander around in an endless maze of your own psychoses until you give up and bash your head into the wall until your skull breaks."

"What? Really?"

He inclines his head. "You are the one who is thinking about violence," he says. "I was only extrapolating to a self-evident conclusion."

"Maybe I don't like your conclusion," you say.
Go to C-74.

"Now you're just trying to wind me up," you say.
Go to C-84.

C-94

Dr. Nebs indicates the door. "Go right ahead," he says.

You get up. You walk out. You go back to the office and submit the paperwork associated with this assessment. And then you go home. Where you take a long hot bath. You drink—probably a little too much—and you go to sleep.

You do not dream, which is fucking marvelous and unexpected.

CONGRATULATIONS. YOU HAVE DEMONSTRATED A HIGH LEVEL OF MENTAL STABILITY IN REGARDS TO YOUR ROLE AS A NIGHT OFFICE CLOSER. A COMMENDATION WILL BE FILED IN YOUR LIFE INTEGRITY EXPERIENCE SCHEMATIC.

MAPS SCORE: 89

YOU'LL BE BACK IN THE ROTATION TOMORROW. DON'T OVER-SLEEP. THE SPACE JELLIES SURE DON'T.

C-95

"No, it's not that," you say.

"It's totally that," Dr. Nebs shoots back at you. "You don't trust yourself, so why should I expect you to trust me."

"I do trust myself."

"Is that why you are trying to hide things from me?"

"I'm not hiding anything."

"Oh? Well what about Alison Cambrie?"

"What about her?"

"Or Hugh Daryrimple?"

"I don't know what you're talking about."

"See? That's the whole problem. You're all walled off from yourself. You are so busy hiding things you've said—things you've done—that you can't allow yourself the time to find someone. Someone to talk to. Someone to open up to. Someone to share your life with."

"Like you?"

"I don't exist, remember?"

"I know, I know."

"Don't brush me off. This is important. You need to trust other people. You need to let someone in."

"Okay, okay. Fine."

He nods and goes back to writing in his journal.

You let him plug away at his notes for a bit, and then you gently clear your throat.

"Yes?" He looks up.

"Are we—are we done here?"

"Sure," he says. He waves his pen at the door.

"That's it?"

"That's it. Unless you want more?"

"More of what?"

He stares at you. "What do you want more of?"
"I hate it when you do that."
A smile darts across his face.

"If you want validation of yourself, you should explore the Dark Labyrinth," he says.
Go to C-75.

"If you aren't sure this is the right path, you should get a second opinion," he says.
Go to C-26.

C-96

Dr. Nebs waves a hand at the door, indicating you are free to leave. You sit up, but you don't get off the couch.

"We're done here," he says.

"No, we're not," you say. "There's something else."

"There isn't," he says.

"There is. This isn't my first rodeo."

He taps his teeth with his pen. "What do you think is going on?"

"I think you haven't told me everything."

"Neither have you," he says.

"Okay, true. But this assessment isn't just about showing me how to talk to myself. There's something more to be learned here."

"You invented me," Dr. Nebs says. "And that's a fine skill. But I'm a complete fabrication. What if you could use this skill to create . . . a ghost."

"A ghost? What do you mean?"

"A relic of someone else. Someone who is no longer alive."

"Like an old grandpa or something?"

"Or something. Does that bring them back?"

"Back from where?"

"From the dead."

"That's—that's not possible."

Dr. Nebs raises his shoulders. "Really? At this point in your career with the Night Office?"

"Who—why would I do that?"

"You might need someone with a different perspective than I can offer," he says.

You touch your fingertips together. Your brain starts ticking on the possibilities. "How would I learn this trick?"

He indicates the door again. "You have to go a little deeper, Acolyte. You have to find the Way."

You get up and walk to the door. When you grasp the handle, it feels different. Slippery. Like what is on the other side of the door might not be there yet.

You open the door.

Go to C-26.

C-97

Dr. Nebs gives you a smile that reminds you of the way your aunt used to smile when she was trying to keep her mouth shut. This exercise is utterly fabricated, isn't it? You understand its purpose—forcing field operatives to self-assess their own mental states to make sure they are human—but this sort of introspection could end up shattering your psyche. Think of all the nasty things that might come crawling out of the dark dungeons of your mind.

They need to know if you can handle it, someone says.

You look up. Dr. Nebs is still in his chair, but he's caught in a beam of light. As if he was a projection and someone has just pushed PAUSE on the playback.

Over here.

You look over at his desk. An old man—the Old Man—is sitting in the leather chair. His feet are on the desk. He's got an apple in one hand and a knife in the other. As you watch, he cuts a slice off the apple and eats it.

"You."

It's been boring without me, hasn't it? your old mentor asks.

"It's been . . . different," you say.

That's very politic of you, he says.

"I've learned a thing or two."

He cuts another slice of apple. *Do you want me to tell you about the secret back door?*

"I assume that is why you are here."

He shows you his teeth when he smiles. It's definitely him. No one else grins like that.

I can't tell you outright, he says. *That would be cheating.*

"That hasn't stopped you before."

He shrugs. *Nor can I tell you which path will be more useful.*

"Of course you can't. That would actually be helpful."

Nor can I provide assistance once you pick a path.

"Wow. So many rules. Are you done yet?"

Almost. He cuts another slice. Then he turns the knife around in his hand and offers it to you. He raises his eyebrows.

You look at the frozen form of your therapeutic personality. There is a glimmer of something in your therapist's eyes. Fear? Anger? You're not sure. You're also not sure who froze him. Was it you, or was it the Old Man?

"Am I supposed to take the knife?" you ask.

The Old Man nods at the door behind him. *The lady or the tiger,* he says. *Such a classic dilemma. Always reliable.*

You approach the desk. The knife is a switchblade. Yes, good and classic. Always reliable.

The Old Man grins around a mouthful of apple. He waggles his hand, teasing you with the knife. *Which path will you take?*

You take the knife.

"The lefthand path," you say. You head for the door.
Go to C-26.

"The righthand path," you say. You go back to the couch.
Go to C-23.

C-98

The image forming in your head expands. It fills the room. It pushes the furniture out of the way. You can't see the white painting any more.

That's right. You're doing great. Just a little more. Give it some shape. Give it some color.

It's a path of pale cobblestones, isn't it? Not very wide, but wide enough. As you concentrate on the stones, they take on more color. You think they are safe to walk on now.

You stand and start walking along the path. There is a grinding sound behind you, but you don't look back. The path forms ahead of you as you walk. Very good. Keep your focus. You're almost there.

Now, build something else. Something that will transition you properly to somewhere else. See it in your head before you make it. That's right! A door.

It's a simple door. White. A silver door knob. It's standing in front of you. There's no frame. There's no walls around it. There aren't even any hinges. That's okay. You know it is a metaphor. All you have to do is open it.

Go to Section G.

C-99

The white oil paint bubbles out of the frame. It covers the therapy couch. It drips off onto the floor. It is like the painting has transformed into an artestian spring, a bubbling source of nothingness that will slowly fill the room.

You move back from the couch, a little cautious of the fluid nothingness. That's probably wise. The nothing spreads across the carpet—not very quickly, of course, because Dr. Nebs has very plush carpet in his office. When the nothing reaches one of the legs of the couch, the piece of furniture shifts, as if the nothing won't support any weight.

The pool expands, and the couch tips. As you watch, the couch slides down, vanishing into the nothingness.

The painting was on the couch. It was the source of the nothing, but the nothing has just swallowed the canvas.

Nice paradox, the Old Man notes dryly in your head.

All sorts of things are possible in a paradox. You take a deep breath and jump off the edge of the disappearing carpet, plunging into the nothing.

Go to Section F.

C-100

You take the boxes out of the closet and bring them over to the couch. The first one is a lacquered box with a gold flower inlay. Its lid fits snugly. The second box is a metal box that has been dropped down a flight of stairs or two or twelve. It has a simple hasp lock on it. The third box is covered with paper-maché. The only opening is a narrow slit at the top.

They all rattle, some more dully than the others.

Dr. Nebs is still dead, by the way. Aren't you going to pause a moment and feel bad about that?

While you are hesitating, caught between wondering what you did (and when you had the time, frankly!) and what might in the boxes, the phone on Dr. Nebs's desk rings once.

You hold your breath.

It rings a second time.

The speaker pops and the voice of Dr. Nebs's assistance fills the room. "The moon is full," she says. "The tide has risen. The Deep Ones are coming."

You're out of time. Time to choose before someone else does.

Wrestle open the lacquer box.
Go to C-101.

Pop the hasp on the metal box.
Go to C-103.

Shake the paper maché box ferociously.
Go to C-105.

Leave the boxes. You're not an Opener.
Go to C-110.

C-101

You pry off the lid to the lacquer box. Inside is a single marble—no, wait. It's a prosthetic eyeball. A blue one. It reminds you of someone . . .

That's part of your past that you can't go back to, so it is best to leave those memories alone. "I'm sorry, Archer," you whisper.

You slip the blue eye in your pocket. *It's not a trophy,* you tell yourself.

Something bangs against the door out of the office. You're out of time. You need to find a way out of here.

Maybe you can do something clever with that painting in the closet.
Go to C-122.

Time to bust out the window and make a desperate break.
Go to C-112.

C-102

You close your eyes and imagine another time and place. You try to summon up an image of the room. The colored bedspread. The posters on the wall. Rain beating against the window pane. You've got candles lit, don't you? You can almost smell them.

There's something knocking. It's persistent. It's keeping you from—where is that sound coming from?

You look around. The walls are shivering, as if they were wet paint that is in a rush to dry. The roof ripples and buckles in the corner of your vision. Why can't you focus?

The knocking sound is coming from the closet. The door is closed. But that's not what makes your heart race. This room— this place in your memory—it didn't have a closet with a door. Not like that. This room had accordion doors. This is a different closet.

This is a different room.

In fact, now that you look around in a panic, there is no other door. There is no way to leave this room, except for the window.

The rain lashes harder against the window. The curtains are drawn, so you can't see the weather. You can't see what is outside the room, but in concert with the *knock-knock-knocking* on the closet door, the rain suddenly takes on a more ominous tone. Like perhaps it isn't rain at all. Perhaps it is something else . . .

This isn't helping. Try some other technique. Don't you have another happy place you can go to?
Go to C-26.

If there is a monster out there, it's either already in your head—which is bad. You might as well face it.
Go to C-121.

C-103

You flip open the hasp on the metal box and open it. Inside is an old pocket watch. The second hand is sweeping round and round like time is trying to bite its own tail. You feel a little queasy as you hold the watch, and the light is starting to smear.

The office door opens in slow motion. You are in a bubble of time that is moving at a different rate than the rest of the world. Something with horns and fierce spikes is filling the door. Some kind of nightmare.

Squeeze the watch tighter. Maybe you can make time run even faster.
Go to C-104.

Throw the watch at the thing in the door. Maybe it'll slow it down. No, wait—
Go to C-106.

BEYOND THE WALLS OF SANITY

C-104

You squeeze the watch, and time speeds up. The thing in the door ticks forward, one frame every dozen heartbeats. You can see every fleck of spittle quivering on its slavering jaws. It is a slumbering earthquake that will arrive in a later eon. Before it can rumble all the way into the room, you've already slipped past it. You are gone before it can apprehend that you have left.

The watch is hot in your hand. You can't hold it much longer.

Just a few seconds more.
Go to C-114.

Ditch it. You've got enough of a head start.
Go to C-116.

C-105

You shake the paper maché box vigorously. There's definitely something in there. Sounds like a quarter. You hold the box at an angle so that you can see down in it through the slot. Something glints in the box. Not a quarter, you think.

You shake the box again.

It doesn't make a sound.

Look in the slot again.
Go to C-117.

What the hell? Is it stuck?
Go to C-118.

C-106

You throw the time-dilating pocket watch at whatever is in the doorway, and as soon as the timepiece leaves your hand, you realize your mistake. Whatever is in the time field moves faster than the rest of the world, not the other way around.

Wow. There's no way you can escape now.

The thing in the doorway galumphs into the room. It eagerly slurps into the dilation field and you have only a sec—

WELL, NOT EVEN THAT MUCH TIME.

AT LEAST YOU WON'T REGISTER ANY PAIN BEFORE IT VIVI-SECTS YOU A COUPLE THOUSAND TIMES.

MAPS SCORE: 33

C-107

"I need to get out of this—this labyrinth," you say.

Dr. Nebs looks surprised. "Already? But we've barely started."

"I am going in circles."

"Oh, wait until you get in the Dark Labyrinth," he says.

"I'd rather not. Is there any way to avoid it altogether?"

"You can't. It's a mandatory part of this assessment."

"I thought this was supposed to testing my psychological stability. If I'm stable, why do I need to visit the Labyrinth?"

"Who said you were stable?" He counters your protest. "You're the one who thinks they are going round and round."

"You're confusing me on purpose."

"Of course I am," he says. "What's the point otherwise?"

"But you're a mere project—"

"Not mere," he says. "I'm a rather considerable projection."

"Fine. Whatever. You're still a projection. You shouldn't be able to confuse me like this."

"Well, you're just confusing yourself, so that's like saying that you aren't smart enough to be you."

"I'm not," you protest.

He starts to argue with you, but then he realizes he's about to invoke a paradox. "Now you are confusing me."

"Well, I guess we're both fucked."

"No," he says. "You are. Twice over."

"That's not helping."

He spreads his hands. "Oops."

"Well, I guess I might as well get this over with," you say. You spread your arms to indicate the room. "How do I get into the Dark Labyrinth?"

Go to C-75.

C-108

Though, at this point, you're somewhat used to not being told the rules. If you (and the Night Office) know all the rules, then humanity would be able to tell all those monsters lurking in the Outer Darkness to piss off, once and for all. But, alas, such is not the case. The rules are—well, maybe even the Great Old Ones don't know the rules. The point is: yes, the game is rigged, the decks are stacked, and the odds are long. But that's when humanity does its best work, isn't it? When there is absolutely no chance in hell of survival.

We don't like being told that something is impossible.

Space jellies hate this about us, by the way.

With that in mind: wipe your tears away, buckaroo, and get the fuck back in the game. The Night Office needs you.

YOU MAY TAKE THE WEEKEND OFF. TRY NOT TO HAVE A HANG-OVER ON MONDAY WHEN YOU RETURN TO THE ROTATION.

MAPS SCORE: 57

C-109

"Funny stories are very subjective," Dr. Nebs says. "In fact, a key commonality among Night Office employees is that they don't relate well to others. That makes comedy hard."

"Unlike, say, pathos, which is pretty easy around here."

He looks at you for a moment, his eyes somewhat blank. "Is that a joke?" he asks.

"I thought it was."

He tries to laugh, but all he can manage is a tiny wrinkle in his lips.

"This is a sad reflection on my mental state, isn't it?" you note. "Given that you are me, and I am you."

"You don't laugh much, do you?" Dr. Nebs says.

"Not much to laugh about."

"Yet you just made a joke."

"It was more of a biting comment than an actual joke."

"Mordant humor is a means of communicating in situations that are rife with stress and tension," Dr. Nebs points out. "If you can all laugh at the worst of humanity, then at least each of you isn't alone."

"That's a terrible bit of pop psychology."

"If it works . . ."

"You're saying that I need to work on my people skills."

"Well, it couldn't hurt," he says.

"Will it get me out of this session?"

"Are you willing to admit you are hurting and lonely?"

"Sure," you say. "Whatever."

"Good enough," Dr. Nebs says. He makes a note in his journal. "I'll schedule you for some social skills group sessions."

"That sounds terrible."

"You'll be out of rotation until the sessions are done . . ."

"Will I still be on payroll during this time?"

"Of course."

"Sign me up. What's the worst that could happen in these sessions?"

"You could make a new friend . . ."

You hesitate, suddenly weighing the choice between social skills group sessions and going back into rotation—back into the field. "Do I have to decide right now?"

THE NIGHT OFFICE IS FILLED WITH TOUGH NUTS TO CRACK, WHICH IS A GOOD SURVIVAL MECHANISM.

HOWEVER–AND WE MEAN THIS COMPASSIONATELY–A FRIEND OR TWO WOULDN'T HURT.

MAPS SCORE: 71.

C-110

Ignoring the boxes, you head for the door in the office, but you stop before you open the door. You'll have to walk past his assistant if you go out that way. If she's sending the doc messages about the Deep Ones, she's probably been co-opted. You won't be able to escape that way. You have to find another way out.

You let your gaze roam around the room.

(he's still dead, slain by your own hand when you weren't paying attention)

There's the closet, but it's a dead end, unless . . . unless you can do something clever with that painting.

Or the window. You're only a few floors up. The fall won't kill you.

(especially if you're already dead)

Maybe you could . . . oh, the window doesn't open. You'll have to break it. That'll make a lot of noise.

Well, it's not like you're sticking around anyway. They can bill the Night Office for the window.

Go to C-112.

Maybe something a little less noisy. Perhaps you could use the painting to—who knows?—hypnotize yourself out of this scenario or something.

Go to C-122.

C-111

"That's a serious accusation," Dr. Nebs says. "Do you have any proof?"

"You know what I know. That's all the proof you need."

He considers this for a moment. You notice his leg is wiggling. "I think—" he starts.

"Indeed," you say, cutting him off.

You smile. He smiles back. You both know you have been cheating.

"There are no shortcuts," he says.

"No?" Then how did I end up here?"

Dr. Nebs has no answer to that.

THIS IS UNEXPECTED. YOU MAY EXIT THIS ASSESSMENT WHILE WE CONSIDER HOW YOU ACCOMPLISHED THIS END.

MAPS SCORE: N/A.

C-112

You shove Dr. Nebs's corpse out of the chair. It's not as heavy as you'd like (the chair, not the corpse), but it will have to do. You pull back the curtains so they don't get in the way, and you twirl around a couple of times before launching the chair. It crashes through the window with a satisfactory burst of glass.

The wind rushes in, bringing with it the noise and smell of the street.

Someone rattles the doorknob. "Dr. Nebs?" It's his assistant. "Are you—" The voice changes. "Are you flaying the patient? Are they screaming?"

Well, there's confirmation that you made the right choice.

Time to go, you think as you rush at the broken window. If all of this is a mental simulation, then you should be able to change the landscape with a thought. You don't know how to do it, but you figure if some part of your brain knows, well, it'll tell the rest of you during the three and a half second fall.

You get up some speed, and planting your foot on the couch, you launch yourself through the window. A shard of glass, jutting out from the frame, catches you in the arm. You hear cloth rip. You feel blood on your arm.

Falling, you try to clear your head. *Just one thought,* you tell yourself. One place. One idea. That's all you need.

The ground rushes up fast.

You think about books and then . . .

Go to Section F.

C-113

"But if you don't fill out the paperwork, you fail the assessment," Dr. Nebs argues. He has a stack of documents in his hand. "It won't take long."

"It always takes longer than you say it does."

"Well, that's because you insist on reading all the fine print."

"Only a fool doesn't read the fine print."

He drops the paperwork on his desk. "You should get started." He puts his pen on top of the stack.

With a sigh, you go over to his desk and start filling out the paperwork.

YOU ARE RIGHT. IT DOES TAKE LONGER THAN YOU EXPECT. STILL, IT'S A CONCLUSION TO AN ASSESSMENT THAT ISN'T GETTING EATEN, ABSORBED, TORCHED, LIQUIDATED, ASSIMILATED, OR OTHERWISE SHREDDED. THAT'S A WIN.

MAPS SCORE: 60

C-114

Your hand is burning. You can smell flesh sizzling. But you can't let go of the watch yet. Not until you are out of the building.

You run for the stairs. The lights in the stairwell are flickering slowly, and you see actual shadows in between each flicker. Some of them have teeth in them.

Smoke is rising from your fist now.

You make it to the ground floor, and you burst through the stairwell door. Almost there. As you dash across the lobby, the watch catches on fire. You have to get rid of it.

Just before you reach the turnstile door, you drop the watch. You are halfway through the door when time slows down. You bounce off the glass wall in front of you, leaving a splotch of blood.

Time goes back to normal speed.

You stumble out of the turnstile, out of the office building . . .

Go to Section F. When prompted, please select F-3.

C-115

"Don't be so dramatic," Dr. Nebs says. "No one ever died from paperwork."

"The Night Office doesn't report on any deaths within the organization," you point out. "So, technically . . ."

"Okay, fine. No one *you know* has died from paperwork."

"But I don't have any friends here, so—again—how would I know?"

Dr. Nebs drops the stack of paperwork on his desk. "Fine," he says. "You probably won't die doing all this paperwork."

"Well, I'm not doing it," you say.

"But you have to in order to finish the assessment."

You stretch out on the couch. "You do it," you say. "You're the helpful therapeutic personality. You know everything I know. Make yourself useful. I'm taking a nap."

EFFICIENT USE OF MENTAL BIFURCATION.

MAPS SCORE: 76

C-116

You throw the watch aside, and it catches fire as soon as it leaves your hand. Time suddenly slows down, and your fingertips tingle as the flaming watch vanishes in a burst of light and heat.

Somewhere, several floors above you, a creature howls with displeasure. It's going to find your scent in a minute. Keep moving. Find your way out.

Go to Section F.

C-117

You peer into the slot, trying to spot the glinting thing you saw a minute ago, but the angle is all wrong. Or the light is all wrong. Or . . .

There's something in the box.

You try to throw it again, but a gray pseudopod darts out of the box and wraps around your wrist. Its touch burns. You try to pry it off, but a second tentacle forces its way out of the paper maché box and grabs your other wrist.

Whatever it is, is strong. It tightens its grip, twisting about your wrists. Your flesh steams. The slot in the box is slowly being cranked toward you. You can't get away from it. As soon as that slot faces you, something is going to come out. You know it is . . .

SPACE JELLIES LIKE TO HIDE IN THE CREVICES OF YOUR MIND. THEY ALSO LIKE TO LURE PREY WITH FAKE SHINY. YOU SHOULD HAVE REMEMBERED THIS . . .

MAPS SCORE: 41

C-118

What happened to that quarter. Did it get stuck on something in the box?

You are about to shake the box again, when you feel it shift in your hands. Like something inside the box moved—something larger than a quarter.

You throw the box across the room. It hits the far wall, sticks for a second, and then oozes down, leaving a trail of dark slime on the wall. There was a space jelly in that box!

You need to get out of here before it can force its way out of its small prison.

Make a break for the door.
Go to C-120.

Find some way to break the window.
Go to C-112.

C-119

After you open the portal, you realize you have unwittingly allowed—

THIS RESPONSE IS THE SORT OF WISH FULFILLMENT THAT A SPACE JELLY WOULD INSERT INTO YOUR BRAIN.

IF YOU BELIEVE YOU ARE SUPPOSED TO BE READING THIS, YOU HAVE BEEN LED HERE BY A SUBLIMINAL DIRECTIVE. THAT MEANS SOMEONE IS TELLING YOU WHAT TO DO.

YOUR MIND IS NOT YOUR OWN. PLEASE CONFESS YOUR LACK OF SELF-CONTROL TO AN ADMINISTRATIVE AGENT.

MAPS SCORE: -10.

C-120

You run for the door. The paper maché box jumps and bumps on the floor. You fumble with the doorknob. It doesn't want to turn; it's almost like there is someone on the other side.

You pull the door open, and Dr. Nebs's assistant lets out a shriek. She's standing right outside the door. "I'm sorry," she says, her face flushed and surprised. "I didn't realize—"

Something lands on your shoulder. You know what it is. That greasy, slippery touch of a space jelly.

The assistant's eyes get big.

That same slippery, greasy feeling is in your ear, forcing its way deeper into your ear canal. You feel a mounting pressure inside your head . . .

SPACE JELLIES LIKE COMING IN THROUGH YOUR EAR. IT'S A QUICK ROUTE TO YOUR BRAIN, WHICH IS VERY TASTY.

MAPS SCORE: 27

C-121

You get up from the bed and approach the closet. The knocking continues. You grab the door knob and yank the closet door open.

Dr. Nebs stumbles out. He's been tied up with heavy rope. A sock has been stuffed in his mouth. He bumps into you and then falls down in the middle of the room.

There is a brown smudge on the inside of the closet door. Dr. Nebs has been kicking the door.

You pull the sock out of your therapist's mouth. Dr. Nebs sputters and spits. "Why did you have to shove me in such a dark place?" he complains.

"I don't think it was me," you say.

"Who else could it have been?" He wriggles on the floor, looking like a fish out of water. "Untie me. This is so embarrassing."

The knots are tight and complicated. It will be easier

(don't you remember tying those knots?)

to cut them. You still have the knife, don't you?

The blade snicks out when you press the button. Dr. Nebs freezes when he hears that sound. "What—what are you going to do with that?" he asks nervously.

"I'm going to cut you—"

He starts shrieking and thrashing. It's going to be hard to get at those knots with him throwing himself about like this.

Just stab him already.
Go to C-123.

Wait for him to calm down.
Go to C-124.

C-122

You take the painting over to the couch, where you place it on the cushions. Kneeling, you try to put everything out of your mind as you stare at the white canvas. Breathe. Don't think about anything that might be happening outside this room. Don't think about what might be happening in a reality beyond this one. You're in an imagined reality. You made this. It's part of the process. You can turn it into something else. You just have to focus. You just have to formulate that new world in your mind.

Start with the blank canvas. That's right. Start with something like this: white and uncomplicated. There are no

(rabbits in snowstorms)

shadows in this painting. It's a white expanse. Empty. Pure. That's right. You can imagine a path out of this, can't you?

An image is starting to form in the paint. What is it?

It's exactly what you think it is.
Go to C-98.

It's not what you thought it was going to be.
Go to C-99.

C-123

You kneel on Dr. Nebs, holding him in place. The first cut is easy. After that, things get a little messy . . .

KILLING YOUR THERAUPETIC PERSONALITY WASN'T THE GOAL OF THIS ASSESSMENT. EVEN IF IT DID ANNOY YOU.

MAPS SCORE: 48

C-124

Dr. Nebs is a reflection of your own mental state, and after an hour of listening to him carry on and thrash about on the carpet, you start to wonder if perhaps there's more going on in your head that you've been willing to admit. If Nebs is this freaked out, aren't you as equally freaked out?

Perhaps that was the point of all this. Giving you an opportunity to acknowledge how freaked out you are by what you do for the Night Office.

WE UNDERSTAND. WE'RE KIND OF FREAKED OUT TOO. HOWEVER, WE STILL NEED YOU TO SHOW UP FOR WORK TOMORROW. GET IT TOGETHER, WOULD YOU?

MAPS SCORE: 65.

SECTION D

THE OUBLIETTE

This section has been removed as
per HAND Direction 43/2/ae. Please
disregard any instructions for
SECTION D material and proceed to
Section C-26.

SECTION E

THE EXISTENTIAL CRISIS

This section has been intentionally
left back, mostly so that you will
wonder about what it might have
contained.

SECTION F

THE DARK LABYRINTH

ENTRY

Imagine a vestibule. Don't worry about how you got here. Ahead of you is a turnstile. There are mirrors all around it, and when you enter it, you are surrounded by an endless cascade of versions of you. All of you are spinning round and round. How many times? You lose track. You think about puking. You think about giving up. You think about that girl you wanted to kiss back in school, but were never brave enough to approach.

What would your life have been like if you had been a bit braver back then? Instead of . . . well, you made other choices, didn't you? Choices that showed you darker paths. Choices that left blood on your hands. Choices that were hard, and which you'll never quite recover from, but that's the burden of being a Night Office field operative, isn't it? You make the hard choices, and you learn to live with the nightmares.

(Get off the merry-go-around)

There's a narrow gap. It's hard to focus with all of your reflections frowning at you, but when you lean back and don't make eye contact with any versions of your self, you can see it. You just have to time it right. Feel the rhythm of the wheel

(Going round and round and rough)

and make the jump.

You stumble into a large room badly light by a handful of table lamps on the floor. In the gloom, you see lots of books. Like hundreds and hundreds—maybe thousands. They're on shelves. They're in stacks. They're scattered across the floor. Some of them have been arranged into tiny forts by the mice.

It's the lost bookstore of your subconscious, after all. What did you think it was going to look like? There's no librarian on duty here. There's just a lot of awkward pictures in old yearbooks;

abandoned journals, half-filled with awkward sex dreams; and books you meant to read but never got around to.

It's not stress-inducing. Not in the slightest.

Many of the bookcases are too close together, but you think you can squeeze between a leaning pair on your left. Or, on your right, you might be able to thread your way between stacks of moldering hardbacks.

Upon closer examination, that gap on the left is too narrow. The bookcases look like they could topple over with just a nudge. Maybe it's better to serpentine though the stacks in the aisle on the right.

Go to F-1.

You've been watching your weight these last few weeks, haven't you? You should be able to squeeze through that gap on the left.

Go to F-2.

You know? Neither route looks all that appealing. And why are you here? Shouldn't you figure that out first? This is your imagined reality. You should be able to go back.

Go to F-3.

F-1

You've been in lots of bookstores like this, haven't you? Where the shelves are so overstocked that books are piled on the floor. In many places you can't even see the bottom shelf. Not that you were reading spines, of course. Now is not the time to be shopping, even if you are seeing things like Neudekker's *Nocturnal Practices Among Appalachian Evangelicals* and Nyquist's *Ritualism and Paradox*.

That Nyquist looks like a first edition too.

No! Don't get distracted by the books. You're trying to find your way out of here.

You reach an intersection. The path on your right is less cluttered.

Yes, but there are probably some really good books down the lefthand path. Look at all those stacks on the floor!
Go to F-4.

Stay focused. Stick to the less-cluttered path.
Go to F-5.

F-2

You approach the gap between bookcases. Wow. It is smaller than you thought. You suck in your gut, bend your knees slightly, and start sidling between the angled bookcases.

You're about a meter in when the bookcase in front of you shifts. You stop and hold your breath. Dust swirls around you.

The bookcase wobbles for a second. It is nearly touching your head. You crouch a little bit more and—

Your butt pushes against the case behind you and it moves. Both bookcases start shifting, their wooden frames grinding against one another.

Move! You're running out of time. Push on through!
Go to F-10.

Use your arms and legs to brace the shelves. You've got to stop these bookcases from shifting any more. You can do it.
Go to F-11.

F-3

You turn around and walk through the door. For a minute, everything slips sideways on you. You think about vomiting, and then you think about clawing your eyeballs out. You settle for screaming. Once you're done being hysterical, you settle down and figure out where you are. You're . . .

. . . still in the bookstore.

Well, a bookstore. This one is different than all the others.

(There are others?)

And when you turn around, you discover the door you came through is no longer there.

Great. You are back *here* again.

You eye the aisles in front of you. There are two. Neither look inviting. You figure both are going to be non-linear in their path. You try to get excited about the idea of finding your way out of this bizarre labyrinth. You're dreaming all of this, aren't you? Can you dream a shortcut?

How about a map? Maybe there's a map here somewhere.
Go to F-6.

Take the lefthand passage. It's the only way to deal with this meta-cognitive bullshit. Head on. Be aggressive. If Theseus could manage it, so can you. He wasn't the brightest of the bunch . . .
Go to F-7.

That leaves the righthand path, but that seems almost too easy, too inviting. Don't fall for that trap. Find that shortcut.
Go to F-8.

F-4

You weave between the stacks of books, trying not to knock any of them over. Not because you're worried about making a mess—this place hasn't been cleaned in, well, forever. No, you're more concerned about making noise. Even though this is a construct fabricated by your own damaged psyche, that doesn't mean there aren't strange beasties roaming around.

Also: think positive thoughts. Just in case.

Anyway, you dodge from side to side, finding a rhythm. You feel like a true bookworm, easing back and forth. Eventually you reach a small open space, almost like a rest stop. There is a chair here (though a stack of books are piled on its seat), and opposite it, there is a gap between bookcases. You look through the gap and see another aisle.

A little rest sounds nice. You can move those books off the seat of the chair.

Go to F-13.

You eye the chair suspiciously. While it might be comforting to sit down for a few minutes, you hesitate. How hard is it going to be get up again? Not physically, but emotionally? You can't overlook the mental strain you are under.

Go to F-14.

F-5

You stick to the less-cluttered path. What's the line from that great Americana poem? "I took the path less traveled," or something like that. Take the path less cluttered. This is your mind, after all. Clutter is what got you in trouble. Too much thinking. That's how the space jellies got you.

Well, they haven't gotten you yet. That's the point. If they had, you wouldn't be wandering around your own head. Your personality matrix would be shredded. There'd be little left of "you," and lots of "it."

Stop thinking. Keep moving. Don't let your memories overwhelm you.
Go to F-4.

It's okay. Take a deep breath. A little introspection now and again won't hurt anything. But not too much.
Go to F-15.

Hey, three left turns. Careful there. Isn't this upcoming left turn going to loop you back to where you've already been?
Go to F-7.

F-6

You dig around in the stacks for awhile, and while you find a number of childhood classics you had forgotten about in the last several decades, you don't find a map. It was a long shot anyway, wasn't it? Having a map of the Dark Labyrinth sort of defeats the whole purpose of a confusing conundrum intended to sap your will.

You're about to give up on this nonsense when you uncover a copy of Bergele's *Incandescent Mythology*. You haven't seen one of these in a long time. You could never afford a copy of your own, but the Rare Book Room at the university had one, and you recall wrangling a note from one of your instructors to get access to the room. Ostensibly, you were supposed to be reading Chaucer, but you convinced the TA who worked the RBR desk that you were doing a thesis on Medieval Oratory Incantations, didn't you? You were attempting to draw parallels between Chaucer's accentual-syllabic verse and cosmological invocation chants used by pagan cults of the same era (as noted in Bergele's book).

It was all nonsense, of course, but as you suspected, the TA had no idea what Bergele's book was actually about.

As you open the copy of *Incandescent Mythology* that has found its way to your Dark Labyrinth, a slip of paper falls out. At the top of the page is the university's logo. There's a number scrawled on the page, and it takes you a moment to recall how the on-campus phone directory worked.

PS3523. Oh, right. The TA slipped you their number.

Funny how you've forgotten that relationship. Well, it didn't last long, in any event.

Anyway, it doesn't look like there is a map. Just this sad reminder of one of your failed attempts at human contact.

PS3523. You doubt the number works anymore. Even if it did, that person won't live there. Let it go.

Well, that was a waste of time.
Go to F-17.

This is going to take some persistent effort and maybe even some sustained focus. Good thing you're a Closer. You got this.
Go to F-9.

F-7

It's likely that every choice here is the wrong choice, but let's not get wrapped up in that, shall we?

Anyway, the floor isn't very dusty, almost as if someone has been here recently. Either you're already circling back on your own tracks, or you're not alone. The latter makes the back of your neck prickle. This is your mental construct; there shouldn't be anyone else in here. Unless, of course, you have been infiltrated by a space jelly, in which case this is all some kind of sadistic game because you're never going to find your way out. Your body isn't yours anymore.

This is what Dr. Nebs was talking about. The Dark Labyrinth is where the human mind goes when the body has been co-opted by a shoggoth. Well, gold star for you. Nice to validate that Night Office psychological theory.

This job sucks, doesn't it?

You reject this sort of thinking. It's the downward side of a slippery slope. You have to think positive thoughts. Like: *oh, look, this path isn't nearly as dusty and the stacks aren't nearly as high.* There. See? Things are looking up already.

Go to F-5.

Of course the job sucks. How many times were you warned? More than enough. And yet, you persevered. Why? Because you like pain? No, because you think the world is worth saving.

You're such a fool.

Go to F-16.

F-8

You wander back and forth in the lobby here, trying to figure out if there is a way through this labyrinth that isn't blindly following the paths. You test the shelves on a few bookcases, and realize they aren't strong enough to support your weight. Even if they were, your weight is likely to topple the bookcase over, and then you'll be trapped. Pinned like an overeager bibliophile who tried to get a book slightly out of reach.

No, it's got to be the paths. You can't skip off—

Hang on, is that a gap between bookcases? It is, isn't it? Maybe if you shove *this* one to the left a bit. Yes, and then *this* one to the right. Yes, yes. You can squeeze through. That's it. Don't worry about that nail sticking out—

Oh, well, maybe it isn't *that* rusty . . . The bleeding will stop in a bit, won't it? It should.

You're behind the bookcases now. It's very dusty, and here and there you find a crumpled mass that might have been a book once, but dust and time have turned it into something neither alive nor dead. You hurry on, just in case these things release spores or a noxious gas.

The way is narrow and getting narrower. Your sleeve is sticky with blood. The bleeding hasn't stopped, has it? The dust is clinging to your sleeve, soaking up the blood. Like it is thirsty.

Keep moving. Keep stepping over the lumps.

They aren't books. You want to think they are, but you know otherwise. They were other things—maybe people, maybe monsters—and this dust is changing them. Slowly devouring them. Condensing. Coalescing. Forming.

You turn a corner and oh no! A dead end.

There's a body here. It's only been dead for a few hundred years. The lower half of the body is a fuzzy mass of dust and powder. In another thousand years or so, it will be like the other piles you've seen, well on its way to its final state . . .

That's what happens to everyone who gives up in the Dark Labyrinth, isn't it? Over a few millennia they are reduced and transformed into an old book.

You are going to head back. This shortcut wasn't short, and your cut is . . . well, your arm is heavy. The dust is thick on your sleeve. You are losing sensation on that side of your body. Your body feels wooden.

How many steps? You don't remember. There's no reason to count them, but you do, nonetheless. Something to keep your mind active. Something to make you feel alive.

After awhile, you think *forty-eight*, and that is the last number you remember . . .

SHORTCUTS RARELY WORK OUT. THAT WAS BEEN COVERED IN ORIENTATION & INOCULATION.

MAPS SCORE: 22

F-9

Right. Closers close. They put things back in the boxes. They shut doors on unspeakable things that shouldn't be calling. They interrupt dread rituals. They stop the gates from vomiting all sorts of unseemly monstrosities on an unaware public.

This is your fucking job. It's the only job you've ever loved.

Well, most of the time, you think.
Go to F-17.

Damn right you love this. If you didn't—if you weren't so very good at it—you'd be dead.
Go to F-18.

F-10

So get to it. Shove this bookcase hard. Put those muscles to work. Now is not the time to lament how much you haven't been to the gym lately (or at all). Put your back into it!

The bookcase in front of you doesn't want to move. It likes applying pressure against your forehead. It likes the idea of slowing squishing you. But, eventually—grudgingly—it moves.

·Your arms are shaking from the effort, but you're going to hold one for a few more seconds. Push!

You duck your head and dart to your left. The bookcase groans, and somewhere ahead of you, stacks topple over. Your foot kicks something. You nearly stumble, but you've got momentum now. You can see the light on the other side.

The bookcase clips your shoulder, and you flail and fall, but you've got room for all that nonsense. Luxuriate in the open space.

Behind you, wood groans, snaps, and splinters. The bookcases have closed the gap. You're not going back that way.

Dusting off your pants, you survey the aisle ahead. The shelves bow under the weight of the books. There are stacks all the aisle. The route is narrow, but manageable.

The shifting bookcases have opened up a another gap. It's a narrow squeeze, but it might be a shortcut.
Go to F-19.

Well, it's probably not a good time to start thinking about all the dust in the air. Not to mention the possibilities of what kind of mold is eating some of these books. Better to keep moving.
Go to F-18.

F-11

You straighten your legs and push up with your shoulders. The bookcase behind you is pressing against the back of your head and your neck. You put your arms against the bookcase in front of you. You push hard, trying not to think of that scene in that movie where everyone was caught in a tiny room where the walls were moving in.

Things turned out all right for them, didn't it? But they had friends who figured out which lever to pull. Which button to push. How to reverse the trap.

The closest thing that you have to "friends" are the members of your team, but they're not here right now, are they? You're trapped in your own psyche.

Probably just as well, anyway. After what you did, they might not be terribly friendly. Though, to be fair, you were the only one who saw the danger. You had to do what you did. Otherwise . . .

All that aside, you really need to do something about these bookcases. They're heavy and getting heavier. You're not sure how much longer you can hold them.

This isn't one of those times when you want to be brave and strong. It's time to shove hard and make a break for it, isn't it?

Go to F-10.

You'll hold these goddamned shelves as long as you need to. You're the strong one. You're the one who didn't crack. Everyone else lost their mind. You didn't. And you're not going to now.

Go to F-12.

F-12

Except, you sort of did lose your mind, didn't you? You are the one who took the knife and made that unkind cut, aren't you? Their blood is on your hands. It was so warm, wasn't it? And you were so cold.

Your teeth are chattering, aren't they? Your muscles are starting to quiver. You glance to your left. The edges of the bookcases are less than a meter away. Every time you falter, the gap will close a little more. It won't be long before you can't hold the line anymore . . .

ARE YOU FAMILIAR WITH HOW A PRESS OPERATES? YOU'RE NOT GOING TO GET OUT.

YOU'RE GOING TO BE . . . PULPED.

MAPS SCORE: 27.

F-13

You grab the stack of books on the chair and move them to the floor. You can't help but notice the top book is a weather-stained copy of Killeman's *Spirtual Englightenment Among the Hedge Mazes of the North*. Your aunt had a copy of that book on her shelf. In fact, when you lift the cover of the Killeman, you see her mark on the upper corner of the fly leaf.

Now that's a curious thing, isn't it?

You grab the book as you sit down on the chair. The cushion is as old as the book and a bit lumpy, but it's nice to sit down, isn't it?

I'm just going to read for a few minutes, you think.
Go to F-20.

You tell yourself that you'll get up after you've turned thirty-six pages. That's all you're going to allow yourself. You have to keep moving.
Go to F-21.

F-14

You approach the gap between bookcases. It's wider than the previous gap, and eying the bookcases on either side, you judge that neither is going to suddenly fall over when you squeeze through the gap.

You look back at the chair. You're tired, aren't you? It's been an exhausting few weeks. You're not sure you have the stamina to keep on like this. You need a break.

It won't be a long break, you tell yourself.
Go to F-13.

You can't get out of this mental conundrum if you sit down and read. Reading is what got you into all of this trouble in the first place.
Go to F-23.

F-15

Why did you become a Closer? Not for the glamor, surely. If you are successful, you save the world. If you aren't, well, you're probably dead so it doesn't matter. There's no real middle ground with Closing. You can't half-close a door. You can't half-close a container of ice cream. It's very simple, in that regard.

And even if you post a string of successes, who can you tell? It's not like the Night Office gives out commendations. Got your tenth space jelly? Here's a certificate. Push an Elder Minion back to the non-geometrical space it tried to crawl from? Well done. Here are some steak knives. No, the Night Office doesn't do any of that. In fact, if you succeed, they insist on a psychological workup, because they know you've looked into the Abyss, and surely, the Abyss looked into you.

No one retires from Closing. The best you can hope for is being committed to one of the nice facilities upstate where someone wipes your chin and your ass with fine microfiber cloths. You don't have to worry about putting on pants or appointments or whether it's Toast Day or if you left the stove on. You can fade away on your own time.

The Night Office are cold, but they aren't cruel.

All that aside, why are you here? Because you're the exception to the rule? Because you can make a difference? Because the puking, squabbling, fornicating mass of humanity is worth saving?

What makes you so special?

It's not the best pep talk, but it's not anything you haven't heard before. The Night Office is just like everyone else in your life. They think they know you. But they're wrong, aren't they?
Go to F-23.

It's kind of funny that your own imaginary black iron prison is talking shit, isn't it? Could it be afraid of your determination? Though, to be fair, why your subsconscious mind is worried about your conscious mind is a bit of a brain twister . . .

Go to F-24.

F-16

Thoughts like this are going to creep in, aren't they? That's the whole nature of this place. It is built by Doubt, powered by Uncertainty, and the ambience is provided by Imposter Syndrome. Everything about the Dark Labyrinth is intended to make you think you fucked up. That you've done something wrong. That you need to submit to a higher authority who will judge you (and find you lacking, of course). Its sole purpose is to break you.

Are you going to let it do that?

Heck, no.
Go to F-15.

Well, maybe—no, that's not the right answer.
This is hard, isn't it?
Go to F-17.

F-17

During the sixth week of Orientation & Inoculation, you learned about the Subjective-Objective Disentanglement. When a space jelly gets in your brain, it tries to subvert your Ontological Phenomenological Index, which is to say that it tries to convince your brain that it doesn't understand reality. Of course, your brain is hardwired to a lot a sensory intake systems, which do a pretty bang-up job of recording objective data that validates the existence of reality. However, if an agency can get deep enough, it can shift the OPI. That's what disassociates you from reality. That's the Subjective-Objective Disentanglement.

You don't want this to happen to you.

And so the Night Office teaches you how to be aware of changes to your Ontological Phenomenological Index. They show you how to reset your Subjectivity. They teach you about the Pure Objectivity Persistence—using models provided by Plato's Communion and Descartes' Axiomic Affirmation, for example).

Yes, but can you trust this sort of psychobabble? Isn't this the sort of nonsense a space jelly would fill your head with?

Go to F-24.

Something has got to be *not-true*, otherwise truth has no objective meaning. That's how the Universe comes unraveled, after all, and you don't want to unravel the Universe.

Go to F-25.

F-18

There is a constant *tick-tick-tick* at the back of your brain when you're on a mission, isn't there? That nagging voice is always asking: *Have you lost your mind?* Because it's a fine distinction between a psychotic break and getting lost in the n-dimension where the space jellies swim. Constant vigilance are the watchwords you live (and die) by.

You develop your own litmus tests—markers by which you check, double-check, and triple-check whether you still have one foot in objective reality. Sure, you might let a couple triple-checks slip by, because you do encounter some really strange shit out there in the Way. But failing to bother with double-checks? Oh, that's a sure sign your brain is toast.

Check now. Check again. What do you find?

Everything is fine. You've got this. In fact, there's a narrow gap between the bookcases here. You saw it before, but you weren't sure if it was a good idea. Now that you've double-checked yourself (triple-checking is a luxury you don't have right now), you can risk it. It might be a shortcut.
Go to F-19.

You're not convinced you're making any headway. The Dark Labyrinth is a serious mind fuck. But you have to find your way out if you're going to have any chance of surviving this mission.
Go to F-26.

F-19

Do you know what happens when you take a shortcut while you attempting to unravel your own mental disintegration? You skip a step. It might not seem like much. *Oh, la la la, look at us tripping along.* Except you can't be that lackadaisical. Not with your sanity. You will miss something. Like, the unstable floor right over here.

Oh, whoops. Now you've done it.

ARE THERE SPIKES IN THE PIT YOU JUST FELL INTO? OF COURSE THERE ARE. AND THEY ARE PROBABLY POISONED WITH AN OINTMENT MADE FROM YOUR OWN FAECAL MATTER, JUST TO REALLY DRIVE THE POINT HOME.
SO TO SPEAK.

WHAT AN AWKWARD WAY TO DIE.

MAPS SCORE: 38

F-20

Your aunt doesn't talk a lot about her time in England, but you know enough to keep your eyes open and your mouth shut. You've seen the books on her shelves. She never forbade you from looking at any of them, and after that summer at Harrowroot, there was an unspoken invitation to do so. She wasn't going to teach you. No, she didn't want that responsibility, but she wouldn't stand in your way if you showed any interest.

This was how the Night Office recruited you too, wasn't it? They didn't say no; they merely opened the door and said someone should shut it. You resisted for a while. You didn't want to be belong. You liked being a rebel. You liked being on the outside. But, eventually, that open door was too much. It needed to be closed.

Anyway, you remember your aunt mentioning Killeman—though she called him "Kili," didn't she? And one night, she had let slip that some of that "spiritual enlightenment" was a euphemism for "getting naked in the woods."

We're all so polite about these sorts of things, aren't we? When did that happen?

Oh. come on. There's no reason to lie to yourself here in the Dark Labyrinth. You can't hide from the things you've done.

In fact, the things you've done are written right there on the page in front of you, aren't they? Someone has marked up this copy of Killeman's *Spiritual Enlightenment Among the Hedge Mazes of the North*. Ah, you remember it now, don't you? Taking that permanent marker to your aunt's books. Changing the sigils. Marking out key passages in the rituals. Oh, you were a naughty child. So rebellious. So angry.

And what did that get you? Your aunt threw you out. She struck your name from her mind. There are no reminders of you in her house. And the school has sealed your records, haven't they? If they haven't purged them entirely. Even Dalton, at the bookstore . . .

You don't exist. All you have is the job, and look what you've done with that. You blew it, didn't you? They were all depending on you, and you made such a mess of things.

You can't go back. You can't face what you've done. Better to stay here, in the dark. Among the musty stacks of all your failures.

BE CAREFUL ABOUT NOSTALGIA. IT CAN LEAD TO FEAR AND RECRIMINATIONS. THOSE THOUGHTS LEAD TO GUILT. GUILT WILL KILL YOU.

THERE IS NO ROOM FOR REMORSE IN THE NIGHT OFFICE.

MAPS SCORE: 43

F-21

Your aunt had a relationship with Killeman, though you're not quite sure how that worked. This book was published in 1906, and your aunt, well, she's not *that* old. You suspect she was pulling your leg. She was kind to you, took you in when no one believed in you, but she was also more than a little batty.

A rich but batty aunt sounds great when you are twelve, but when you get older, it becomes less enchanting. Especially when she mistakes you for someone she thinks she had a feud with during the War.

Which War? That's the whole problem. If you're asking that question, you're already half-convinced she's telling the truth.

Anyway, she meant well. She took care of you. She pointed you in the right direction. That meant a lot.

You look at the book in your lap. *This is nostalgia*, you think. Your aunt would fall into fits of nostalgia that would last for hours. One afternoon, she idly pulled a bok from the shelf, and eight hours later, was still staring at its pages. She wasn't seeing the text. She was lost in her own associated memories. Her encounters (real or not) with the author. Where she bought the book. Who she discussed the book with. What rituals from its pages she had performed. And so on and so on.

It is easy to get lost in a book.

Just a few more pages, you think.
Go to F-20.

No, you can't let this happen to you. You need to keep moving.
Go to F-22.

F-22

You shut the book and gingerly put it back on the stack next to the chair. It's hard to let go, and for a minute, you reconsider. Surely a few more minutes won't hurt? It's not like you're in a rush, right?

This isn't a comfortable bookstore. This is a mental prison you've gotten lost in. There are memory palaces and there are psychotic panopticons. Sometimes it is hard to tell the difference, especially when they look like your favorite bookstore.

Your hand is still on the book.

Just one more look, you tell yourself. There's got to be a clue in there.
Go to F-20.

Leave the book. Get out of the comfy chair. You have to keep moving.
Go to F-24.

F-23

You keep moving. That's all you can do. You find your way into another aisle. It looks like the other aisles, though the stacks are smaller and the titles and author names on the spines aren't familiar.

You keep trudging on. You come to another intersection. This one has a pot of dark earth sitting on top of a stack of books. You don't approach the pot because you know nothing good could possibly grow in that dark soil.

You turn a corner and find an aisle with empty shelves. For a moment, you are elated because you haven't seen empty shelves yet. But, as you stagger forward, you realize how much dust is on these empty shelves. Are you going the right way?

You stop and look back. You don't remember the turns you've made. How far back was the pot of dark earth? The answer keeps slipping away from you.

I'm going deeper, you think. You're in a section that is so old the books have turned to dust.

You are completely lost.

THIS IS WHAT THE DARK LABYRINTH WANTS. IF IT CONVINCES YOU THERE IS NO WAY OUT, THEN IT HAS WON.

MAPS SCORE: 24

F-24

If everything around you—the books, the dust, the crushing hopelessness of being lost in your fucking psychosis—is nothing more than a manifestation of your deep-seated fears and terrors, then doesn't it follow that other parts of your psychological and emotional self are here as well? Where's your persistent and perpetually naive sense of hope? Where is your ruthless determination to be your own person? Where's that iron spine that kept you from slitting your wrists or taking too many sleeping pills?

Those parts of you are here too. You just have to find them.

Well, it's not as simple as that. The Dark Labyrinth is a prison created by a frightened and angry part of your subconscious. It's powered by the dark things you have tried to forget. You're not going to find a cute little unicorn in here somewhere that will lead you freedom. That's not how it works.

Go to F-28.

Hang on. That unicorn option sounds like *hope*.
Go to F-27.

F-25

This is like one of those syllogisms they drilled into you.

> 1. *All small dogs frighten me.*
> 2. *Before me is a small dog.*
> 3. *Therefore I must be frightened.*

Because this is a thought experiment, you aren't allowed to argue to validity of any given statement. Each individual statement is true; if it isn't, then the conclusion cannot be achieved through deductive reasoning. Whether or not you are afraid of small dogs is outside the scope of this inquiry and, therefore, cannot be contested.

It's not the best example of logical thinking, but it'll do for our purposes, okay?

Here's another one:

> 1. *All things that come through cosmic gates intend to devour our brains.*
> 2. *You do not wish to have your brain devoured.*
> 3. *Therefore, you must close the gates before the space jellies can get through.*

See? It's as simple as that.

Okay, let's try a couple . . .

> 1. *Space jellies transform a human host by consuming their brain, which results in discordant mental activity and behavior on the part of the host.*
> 2. *You stabbed someone you shouldn't have. Nor is it in your basis nature to do such a thing.*

3. That is aberrant behavior, which means a space jelly is in your brain. It is making you do these terrible things.

Go to F-28.

1. Anything offered as an objective truth by a construct of your own imagination is not true.

2. They—the people in your brain—told you the Dark Labyrinth is real, and that it will devour your brain if you don't escape it.

3. Since those people are lying, the Dark Labyrinth doesn't exit.

Go to F-26.

F-26

It's easy to get yourself tied in mental knots about what's true and what's not, especially when you're wandering around a mental labyrinth that has been fabricated out of your own— well, it might not be *your* fears, but whatever is running the show certainly knows how to manipulate you, doesn't it?

Of course, you could be doing this to yourself, so there's that to consider too.

It's probably best to simplify things to one or two simple truths that you will anchor your OPI—

Oh, you don't remember what the acronym stands for? That's not a good sign. Is that an indication that you are losing your mind?

You know what the OPI is. Don't let your own uncertainty undercut your resolve.

Go to F-29.

It doesn't matter what the acronym stands for. It's just some jargon invented by some academically-insistent psychologist who wants a tenure track and an invitation to the lecture circuit. Neither of which you care about. Why? Because you're on the job, and that job is saving humanity from brain-eating monstrosities. Stay focused.

Go to F-32.

F-27

There are fewer books on the shelves now. There are no stacks of books on the floor either, which means it's easier to see how thick the dust is in this part of the Dark Labyrinth.

See? You're referring to this place by its institutional name. That's progress, right? You know where you are. You know what this place is. You know what you must do.

(It's not finding a cute unicorn, that's for sure.)

Wait. There are unicorns? Who brought a unicorn? No, wait. There are no unicorns. Stay focused.
Go to F-28.

Unicorns don't exist. The whole idea of tempting yourself with an imaginary unicorn is so . . . What's the word? Whatever. It doesn't matter. Get the fuck out of here. Stay focused.
Go to F-30.

The unicorn's a metaphor, anyway, so there's no reason to get all pissy about it.
Go to F-31.

F-28

You're still lost in the book stacks. You're still thinking about the world outside this place. You're still wishing you had a pet unicorn, even though unicorns don't exist. But wishful thinking means your ego still has attachments, which means you haven't been completely corrupted by foreign influence. There's still time for you to find your way out.

This is excellent news, of course. Now all you need to do is adjust the OPI.
Go to F-29.

You've been so very focused, so very determined to find your way out of this black iron prison. Good job. Just a few more steps, okay?
Well, you hope.
Hope is a human emotion. That means you're still you, right?
Go to F-32.

You don't like unicorns. Therefore, the source of this glee and *whee!* about chubby little horned ponies isn't you. It's something else. Like a space jelly.
You're going to have to deal with this mental infestation.
Go to F-31.

F-29

OPI stands for *Optical Paralectric Ideology*.

No, wait, that's not right. It stands for *Oppositional Parameters Interiority*.

Wait. That doesn't even make any sense.

It stands for *Ontological Paramecium*—

God, you hate acronyms. It's one of the things about the Night Office that is so annoying. Everything has to have a multi-syllabic name, and because all those syllables are a pain in the ass to say all the time, everyone compresses everything to acronyms. And soon, no one remembers what the letters mean, and you're all standing around, spouting nonsense jargon at each other all day.

Speaking of which, it'd be nice to talk to a real person, wouldn't it? Yeah, well, you're still in the Dark Labyrinth, so that's not going to happen. In fact, given that you've gotten all distracted by procedural policies and operative acronyms, you haven't been paying attention to where you've been going.

Do you know where you are? Can you find your way back?

HERE'S ANOTHER ACRONYM FOR YOU: MIA. MEMORIAL IN ABSENTIA.

WHEN THE BODY IS STILL ALIVE, BUT THE MIND IS GONE, NIGHT OFFICE PROTOCOL IS TO DISPOSE OF THE PHYSICAL MATTER AS JUDICIOUSLY AS POSSIBLE. PLEASE REFER TO SECTION 4.18 OF YOUR PALM-PIPE-87/es FOR PARTICULARS.

MAPS SCORE: 28

F-30

You turn a corner and . . . there's a bookcase in front of you. It's an actual dead end.

This is awkward. Should have you have made a left back there instead of a right? Or were you supposed to make two lefts and then a right? Or . . . Whatever. It's hard to keep it all straight.

You notice an object on the upper shelf. It's not a book. You reach for it. It's bristly and rough, but it's also squishy.

It's a unicorn! At stuffed one, actually. At some point in the past, it was left too close to a fire. Its fur, which is made from a polysynthetic blend of industrial chemicals, has melted into stiff bristles. Almost like the backside of a freshly-shaved porcupine. One of its eyes is missing. The other one has melted.

It's been years since you've seen this stuffie. It was your best friend in the whole world. When the fire happened, they got you out, but they didn't get out Snuffles, did they?

No wonder you hate them.

SOMETIMES THESE ASSESSMENTS PROVIDE UNEXPECTED INSIGHTS INTO AN INDIVIDUAL PSYCHE. A FIELD OPERATIVE SHOULD IMMEDIATELY SCHEDULE A–

OH, WAIT. YOU'RE LOST IN YOUR OWN HEAD. YOU CAN'T GET THERAPY IN HERE.

NO, YOU'RE ALREADY IN THERAPY. THIS IS JUST THE PART WHERE YOU . . . HAVE A COMPLETE MENTAL BREAKDOWN.

MAPS SCORE: 22

F-31

This whole thing about unicorns is a distraction. You don't really care one way or another, but the insistence that you should care is pissing you off. Which is good, because anger is a human emotion. If you can get angry, then there's still hope, isn't there?

Though, what's the point of getting angry if there's nothing but your own failures and shortcomings to be angry at?

Ouch. That's a hard thing to face, isn't it?

Though, given where you've wandered in the Dark Labyrinth, there's nothing else here. Just you. And what's left of your mind.

HAVE FUN TOGETHER. WHILE YOU CAN . . .

MAPS SCORE: 29

BEYOND THE WALLS OF SANITY

F-32

You reach an open space. It's unusual, given how cramped all these bookcases have been. You pause for a minute, reveling in the unexpected, but the feeling doesn't last long because it's possible the unexpected is merely the next phase in the Dark Labyrinth's efforts to break your will.

It never ends, does it?

There are three aisles leading out of this space. As you try to figure out which passage to take, you notice there are markings on the edges of the bookcases. You can't quite believe your eyes. They look like . . . catalog markers. But . . . you're not that organized, which means they're probably a trap.

Everything is a trap, you think. You might as well pick one at random.

Go to F-33, F-34, or F35.

Hang on. Let's not be that foolish. Maybe you should apply a little forethought to this. Take a closer look at the markers.

Go to F-33.

What's your gut telling you?

Go to F-35.

F-33

Oh, these marks are Library of Congress Classifications. Great. It's an obscurity trap. Or it's a clue. Or both. God, you hate these. Your subconscious can be so annoying.

All right. What are the choices?

BF1031. That's in the sciences, isn't it?
Go to F-36.

GR3122. It's still the sciences, but not the hard sciences. This is more like . . . Sociology? Maybe. Well, one way to find out.
Go to F-35.

PS3523. This one seems familiar, but not because you remember what this classification is. There's another tickle in your brain.

Oh, man. It's a fine, fine line between "clue" and "trap," isn't it?
Go to F-34.

F-34

This aisle goes on and on. The shelves are stacked with old paperbacks. Pulps, in fact. The old trade magazines of the early twentieth century. This is an amazing collection. You recognize a few names—one leaps out at you, especially—and a resolute calm comes over you. You know these writers. You know the stories they tell. The world thought it was all fiction, but you know otherwise, don't you?

You've found your way through, haven't you? Look at these names. You know them, don't you? Nyarlathotep. Cthugha. Shub-Niggurath. Zoth-Ommog. The Unspeakable One. And the one that everyone knows. Yes, you know these names.

"Finally," you say, spotting a copy of *Weird Tales* from February of 1928. It's in surprisingly good condition.

Something heavy moves behind you, and for a moment, you think it's the being mentioned in the historically relevant story in this issue—"squeezing its gelatinous green immensity through a black doorway"—but it's merely a door materializing.

It's black, of course, and for a moment, you are afraid this end is not the end you want, but is the end they are going to force on you.

Don't let the fear win. Not after all this. Keep moving. Open the door.

Go to Section G.

Wait! Bring the magazine!

F-35

There are fewer shelves on the bookcases on this aisle, because the books are oversized. You stop and look at few and discover they are atlases and encyclopedias of distant and unexplored places. This is a marvelous collection, and you are tempted to linger and look at a few, but you know you have to keep moving.

On your left, you spot something on top of a bookcase. It's a leather journal, and it looks like someone was trying to hide it, but they didn't shove it far enough back. You can almost reach it.

There's a stack of old atlases nearby. Shift them over this way. Now you can reach that journal. Just lean forward a little bit. You've almost got it.

You tug at the journal. You catch sight of the spine. It has a name on it. *Oresti . . .*

One of the atlases slips out of the stack. Instinctively, you grab at the nearest shelf for support. Except that shelf is already over-burdened and it groans when you grab it.

You let go, and now you're falling. The floor is hard, and it's going to hurt when you land, but you should be all right.

Except . . .

You pulled the bookcase toward you when you fell, and now it's coming down too. Right on top of you.

AN EMBARRASING DEATH, BUT SINCE IT HAPPENED IN YOUR OWN MIND, NO ONE WILL EVER KNOW. ON THE OUTSIDE, HOWEVER, WELL, YOU'RE PROBABLY DROOLING. FOLKS ARE GOING TO TALK ABOUT THAT FOR A LONG TIME.

MAPS SCORE: 17

F-36

You duck down an aisle with lots of books with matching spines. You examine some of the sets and see that they are collected works of eminent psychoanalysts. Bleuler, Freud, Jung.

You're in the section of the Dark Labyrinth devoted to the psychological landscape, which is exactly what you're trying to sort out. In fact, you could stop a moment and get a professional's opinion on your condition.

Here's Bleuler, who—oh, right. He's the one who gave us "schizophrenia." He argued that one could never be completely cured of this condition, which means that once you've lost your mind, you might think you've gotten it back, but in reality—and this is the kicker—you haven't.

That's . . . That's an unfortunate take, isn't it?

YOU CAN'T EVER ESCAPE THE DARKNESS, CAN YOU? DAMNIT. THEY'VE BEEN LYING TO YOU ALL ALONG. THERE NEVER WAS ANY WAY OUT OF THIS LABYRINTH. IT WAS ALL A LIE.

MAPS SCORE: 37

SECTION G

WAKE

EGRESS

You find yourself in a quaint little apartment. The blinds are
(nailed down, but don't let that distract you)
drawn, hiding the rest of the world—known or unknown.
The furniture is rustic, but comfortable—much more comfortable than that couch in Dr. Nebs's office.

(you remember him, don't you? Is he still alive?)

There is a bookcase along one wall, filled with old paperbacks.
You have an urge to examine the titles, but boy, you fight that
urge. You've seen enough books for awhile. You're looking for
something else.

A narrow hall leads off the living room. There are several
doors of the hall. The first several are locked. The last door—the
door on the right—is not, and when you open it, you find a
small bedroom.

The bed isn't very big, but it looks—and feels!—comfortable.
You sit on the edge of the bed and consider taking a nap. It's
been a long day

(has it only been a day?)

and you feel like you have a ways to go yet before you can rest.

Though, there is never any rest for a Night Office field operative, is there? They keep working you until you slip up. That's
when you don't come back from a mission.

Funny how you never thought about that part of the Willing
& Ready Invocation form. Sure, some charity will get a nice
donation when you die, but they never have to worry about
notifying next of kin or disposing of a body, do they? No, field
operatives just don't come back.

Sitting on the edge of the bed, you wonder how many don't
come back from this post-operation assessment. How many
field operatives have such a fragile grasp of their own sanity

that the byzantine complications of talking to the therapist is too much for them?

Better to break in-house than when you are in the field, the Old Man offers.

It's a curious side-effect of this assessment that you've created more than one therapeutic personality, though you're not sure you are ready to think of the Old Man as a "therapeutic" voice in your head.

He chuckles, or maybe you chuckle—it doesn't matter. There's no one else to hear it.

You run your fingers along the whorls on the bedspread. It feels like you are rubbing sea shells.

There's no way out of this apartment. You're going to have to dream your way home.

Make yourself comfortable on the bed. *Let's get this over with,* you think.

THIS CONCLUDES THE ASSESSMENT. YOU HAVE SUCCESS-FULLY REACHED THE END.

BASELINE MAPS SCORE: 80

IF YOU WERE GIVEN A GOOD LUCK CHARM: +4 MAPS

IF YOU RETRIEVED A COPY OF BAUDELAIRE'S FLOWER OF EVIL: +4 MAPS

IF YOU RETRIEVED A COPY OF WEIRD TALES (FEBRUARY 1928): +12 MAPS

IF YOU RETRIEVED ORESTI'S SOUTH AMERICAN JOURNAL 1951, VOLUME 3: +16 MAPS

APPENDIX: This Advanced Psychological Strategies assessment captures the current mental state of an Asset Resource Management field operative. It is intended to provide an unbiased assessment of a field operative's capacity to function effectively in the field, as well as assess whether their personality index has been co-opted by a variety of extra-terrestrial entities, cosmic fungi, and other non-Euclidean monstrosities.

In the course of taking this assessment, field operatives receive a Mental Acuity and Psychological Stability score that accurately reflects the choices and decisions they made during assessment. This score is used by Night Office management to determine whether the field operative is sane enough to return to the field.

MAPS scores will be noted on a field operative's Life Integrity Existential Schematic. MAPS scores will be considered during advancement protocols, field operation postings, and other administrative matters as managed by the Human Asset Naturalization Department. MAPS scores may also be taken into consideration during audits by Psychological Investment Notary & Emotional Analysis Legation.

NOTE: Field Operatives who have recently undergone a Wyxstyx-Charbellion Analysis from Labyrinthian Observation & Byzantine Elucidation
may replace any failing MAPS score from this
assessment with their Wyxstyx-Charbellion Index
score, provided that score is greater than 23.

A score of 'N/A' from this assessment indicates
that the field operative has deviated signifi-
cantly from the spirit of this assessment—an
indicator that their psychological matrix is
currently in an advanced state of flux. These
operatives have not failed the assessment.
They have merely demonstrated such a degree of
lateral thinking that this assessment cannot
properly capture their mental state. In these
situations, field operatives are to be placed on
temporary hiatus with the Night Office. They may
retake this assessment in 4 - 6 weeks, provided
there are no incidents of excessive emotional
outbursts, mood swings, chemical dependencies,
destructive relationships, or binge-watching
media programs with no discernible narrative
outcome.

All decisions by Night Office Asset Resource
Management in relation to the results of this
assessment are final.

SCORING: You may have had an opportunity to retrieve an item during aspects of this assessment. Those items reflect the field operative's ability to navigate deep memory correlations. Please add the appropriate bonus to your MAPS score.

0 - 20 > Fail.
Field operative is mentally unstable and is not cleared for further field operations at this time.

21 - 50 > Fragile.
It is highly recommended that the field operative be restricted to menial office duties for 12 - 36 weeks.

51 - 65 > Serviceable. Field operative has suffered some psychological scarring. Cleared for field operations, but should not be placed in a leadership role.

66 - 80 > Satisfactory.
Field operative has demonstrated sufficient mental resilience to continue activities at their current status. It is recommended that they undergo a different APS assessment following their next field operation.

81 - 96 > Excellent.
Field operative has demonstrated a significant resilience to mental duress and psychological assault. A citation of excellence should be forwarded to Topical Human Utilization Management & Benefits in light of this result.

97 + > Psychotic and/or Overly Enthusiastic.
Field operative is exceptionally capable of efficient operation in mental peregrinations that are antithetical, amoral, and highly unethical. Likely to be unable to function as a productive member of society outside the Night Office purview. Keep this one close. The Night Office needs monsters of its own.

CERTIFICATION: Additional certification opportunities are available from the Night Office website. Please visit at your earliest convenience and explore those opportunities.

Sign up for the newsletter to be informed of future educational exercises and training manuals, as well as other occupational possibilities.

www.nightoffice.org

DISCLAIMER: This Night Office Advanced Psycho-
logial Strategies assessment is offered as-is,
and is not indicative of any threat to humanity, real or imaginary, historical or poten-
tial, perceived or dreamt.

Made in the USA
Middletown, DE
26 April 2021